Desperate Writers

WRITE AGAIN

by Margaret, Julia, Ann, Deb

Cover art by Julian Growcott

Produced by:

FriesenPress
Suite 300 – 852 Fort Street
Victoria, BC, Canada V8W 1H8

www.friesenpress.com

Distributed to the trade by The Ingram Book Company

Table of Contents

INTRODUCTION

The Port Alberni Desperate Writers is a group of four women who met at an Elder College Creative Writing class. The name 'Desperate' came about when the writers began to meet once a month and desperately critiqued each other's writings with an eye on future publication.

Soon their collection of material grew and the writers published their first selection of short stories and poems in 2007. The book sold out quickly. Now, the Desperate Writers feel the need to publish again.

Each writer says she was destined to write at an early stage in life. Margaret knew she wanted to be a writer when she won a High School essay competition in Cheshire, England, where she grew up. She immigrated to Canada in 1976 with her musician husband and two children. Margaret does not care for contemporary novels, her favourite author being A. J. Cronin of the '40s and '50s. She also admires famous women writers such as Jane Austen and the Brontë sisters. Although aspiring to be an author of children's stories, on retiring to Vancouver

Island, Margaret found her niche as a freelance writer for a monthly magazine published in Victoria.

Born in Amsterdam, Ann moved to Canada in 1951. Her creative pen has covered every genre of writing. Her favourites are poetry and nonfiction stories which she writes for her great grandchildren, preferably by hand. Ann enjoys L.M. Montgomery and Rosamunde Pilcher.

Julia emigrated from Ireland in 1969. Her time is spent researching and writing family history. She enjoys reading poetry and listening to classical music, and declares the combination helps her put some rhythm and flow into her writing. Julia reads and edits her own writings about 50 times before she submits them to the group for scrutiny and comments. Not all suggestions are accepted, but the process provides the perfect platform on which to build a more easily read and enjoyable piece.

Deb has resided on Vancouver Island since the 1960's. Always a story-teller she decided it was time to put the stories down on paper. Deb enjoys historical fiction as well as the poetry of early writers. She works full time and writes whenever she has a spare moment, all thanks to modern technology!

The Desperate Writers of Port Alberni will continue to write as long as they have stories to tell. Besides daily life, they face the challenges of the computer age. Writing requires time and energy! Once the story is on paper, many hours go into editing and discussion of possible improvements.

The writers hope to put this book into the hands of many people. Short stories and poems are easy to read when you have a few quiet moments.

Enjoy!

MARGARET GROWCOTT

AT THE MARIGOLD CAFÉ

My best friend, Janet, had slipped me an envelope at school.

"Dear Beryl," it began, on the fancy notepaper inside. "Now that I am almost thirteen, I feel I have outgrown birthday parties. Two weeks ago, I had to suffer my little brother's party. It was awful. No more birthday parties at home for me. Instead, I am inviting you to Tea on Saturday afternoon at the Marigold Café."

I discovered that Corinne, my other best friend, had also received the same envelope. And Jennifer Hewitt, too. She was my next very best friend. How simply divine! An invitation to Afternoon Tea, just the four of us, at the Marigold Café! I had been there a few times as my parents always took visiting relatives to the Marigold for lunch.

The Marigold Café and Bakery, one of the oldest buildings in Sandford-on-Sea, faced broadly onto Market Street. It was almost opposite Parade Road which led down to the Promenade. From the Café, which was upstairs over the shop and bakery, you could see the Town Hall, a red brick building, where Town Hall business took place. Right next to it was the Central Hall, where everything else happened: concerts, exhibitions, blood donor clinics, political campaigns, etc. If you leaned out of the Café window, you could see St. Bridget's Church, and beyond that, the Lighthouse. Oh yes! You could see almost everything from the Marigold Café.

Immediately opposite the Marigold Café was the milliner's, Madame Monique Roche, and next door, a dress shop owned by her sister-in-law, Mademoiselle Yvette Roche. My grandmother spent a good deal of her time at both these establishments, so I knew how important and successful they were. Grandma said if you were in there long enough, you could learn pretty good French. I hardly ever went there, although my mother said I should, French not being my best subject.

Squeezed next to these two shops on the corner was Austin's, the kind of shop that sells everything you might need at the seaside: newspapers, books, sweets, ice cream, fishing nets, kites, buckets and spades. It simply overflowed with great stuff. When we were as young as Janet's brother, we had spent a great deal of time in there. But what was most interesting was that buses stopped right outside the Marigold Café; buses to Chester on one side of the street and, on the other side, buses going to Birkenhead. It was amazing who you could see getting on and off these buses. People you sometimes recognized, who went into the Town Hall or the Central Hall. Some went further down Parade Road to the Bank and those with nothing better to do would take a stroll all the way down to the sea.

Saturday finally arrived. I caught the bus from our house down to the shops. It was only half a mile but I didn't want to spoil my new Princess Margaret-style patent leather shoes by walking. It was so nice to escape from our house of hostilities: my Mom and Dad on the warpath with my sister, Molly, who had been out late again. Janet had to put up with her little brother, and Jennifer was an only child. Corinne had an older sister like me, but her sister, although sophisticated, was always nice. She would let Corinne try on all her clothes and high heels, just for fun. My own sister was mean; she was eight years older than me, was going to College, and she acted like a Queen Bee. She would kill me if I set foot in her room.

Once upstairs in the Marigold Café, we sat ourselves down, pulling out the heavy Hepplewhite chairs over the dark, highly polished hardwood floor, and scraping them as near to the table as possible. The damask tablecloth, white as snow, was a good foil for the blue Willow Pattern cups and saucers. Princess Elizabeth and Prince Philip smiled down at us from the opposite wall.

Busy? I should say it was. Other people were taking Afternoon Tea, but we had an almost private room in the alcove of the large oriole window, with a table big enough for a soccer team; so lordly and grand for the four of us. From this vantage point, we could see all the way down to the shore where the foaming waves lashed the pier on that windy October day. The afternoon fish boat was just coming in. Oh yes! We could see everything from the Marigold Café.

On that Saturday afternoon, the bakery was quiet below, already packed up for the weekend. No more machines humming with bread dough and cake mixtures until early Monday morning. The café was closed on Sundays, of course, because nobody did anything on Sunday, except go to church. At least, that's what my father said they should do. So every Sunday, we always went to St. Bridget's and sat in the second pew. The hats were something to see, especially at Easter and Christmas. You could always tell Madame Monique had been kept busy.

As we gazed out the window, the conversation lulled. It was lovely to escape to this haven of elegance and tranquility. All morning I had been witness to a fight between Molly and my Dad. He had been telling her off yet again about Jeff, the apprentice mechanic at Lester's Garage.

"He might be the boss's son," Dad had said for the fiftieth time. "But I don't approve of him. He's got girlfriends here, there, and everywhere. I forbid you to go out with him. You'd better concentrate on your College work. We don't want any more letters about low marks."

The tea was brought – Earl Grey, but I didn't mind. For once I would forego the Orange Pekoe, and I would sip Earl Grey with a thin slice of lemon. Our slim hands and delicate wrists were hardly matronly enough to handle the heavy silver teapot. Janet asked Jennifer to pour the brew. "You've got the strongest arms, Jen. Tennis champ and all."

A platter of dainty sandwiches was placed next to the teapot.

"Oh, look, there's Miss Brocklebank," said Janet as she passed the sandwiches while craning her neck to look out of the window. "Remember? She used to teach us at Elementary School."

"She's going into Madame Monique's," said Corinne, her mouth stuffed full.

"And look who just propped his bike up on the Town Hall railings," said Jennifer, looking at me meaningfully. "It's Jeff Lester."

"Yes, it's him all right." I said, holding out my cup for a refill. "Molly promised Dad she'd finish with him."

The waitress hovered in the background with her black dress, frilly white apron, and funny little white headband, slightly askew. Janet said she was somebody's sister; no one I knew. When "somebody's sister" saw the sandwiches had disappeared, she produced a two-tier plate of little cakes, all different colours. Hot water was added to the teapot. Oh, it was so delicious, the whole thing. Truly delightful. I even thought I was beginning to like Earl Grey tea.

Janet dabbed her napkin to her mouth and then opened her presents with exclamations of delight. She loved my powder puff with its elegant holder. There was a set of satin-covered coat hangers from Corinne, followed by the very latest Enid Blyton book from Jennifer. We were passing them round to each other for inspection when Corinne suddenly pointed out of the window.

"Beryl, isn't that your sister getting off the bus?"

"So it is," I breathed, with a sinking heart. Before our very eyes, Molly ran across the street to the waiting Jeff Lester. With clasped hands and their arms swinging, just as if they were in love, they made off down Parade Road towards the Promenade. I was so sure I'd heard her tell Dad that very morning that she hated Jeff.

What on earth was my father going to say now? I pondered this question whilst sampling a darling little pink cake with nuts on top. But ... did he have to know?

The girls all looked at me. Their eyes said, *don't tell!* A nut seemed to stick in my throat.

Yes, you could see everything from the Marigold Café ... if you wanted to.

THE COCKTAIL PARTY

It was **the** thing to do – go to a Cocktail Party, or host one yourself. It was a month before the Coronation and everybody was dizzy with the idea of it. Celebrations, gatherings, parties, even church services, were all going on in a frenzy. We soon found out, my sister and I, that a Cocktail Party was definitely the "in thing" for our younger set. We were thrilled to be invited to a cocktail party by our elite friend, Bella.

The invitation had come by mail with its demure silver and deckle edge with envelope to match.

LORD AND LADY AYLWARD

On behalf of their daughter, Bella, and son, Nigel

Request the pleasure of the company of

Miss Deirdre and Miss Angela Hargreaves

AT A COCKTAIL PARTY

IN HONOUR OF THE CORONATION

AT ALYWARD HALL, TOSHINGTON

Saturday, May 23rd 1953

4.00 p.m. to 6:00 p.m.

R.S.V.P.

Deirdre and I were crushed to find that our older brother, Charlie, had also been invited (on a separate invitation because he was a boy, I suppose). He could have declined of course, but Charlie was not so shy anymore and was really into the social scene.

Naturally, most girls wanted to emulate the lovely Princess Elizabeth, soon to be Queen of England, having watched her for months on the News at the local cinema, where we saw the pre-Coronation events with the stunning ball-gowns and jewels, each occasion more and more splendid.

Unfortunately, our mother's wardrobe did not run to anything like that, but there were some quite nice gowns huddled at the back, swathed in dust covers. I chose a white brocade sheath dress, which was supposed to be mid-calf length, but because I was nowhere near as tall as my mother, came down to my ankles. The waist had to be taken in a couple of inches. There was a generous slit up one side, but even so, walking was almost impossible unless the dress was hitched up. Mobility was not helped by the stiletto heels that I had never worn before. Being also from my mother's closet, they too were on the large size, but I got around that by adding numerous insoles. Finally, I did manage to balance very well.

Deirdre chose a creation in voluminous sage-green tulle, also courtesy of our mother. The frothy material floated around her calves, and swirled up here and there as she walked, to show a creamy lace-edged petticoat. Her dress had to be taken in at the waist too, and the bodice padded. The plunging neckline demanded to be filled by an imitation pearl choker. The footwear of black, pearl–buckled pumps completed Deirdre's outfit.

My pristine white dress had a mandarin collar requiring no necklace, but Mom had lent me her *faux diamanté* earrings, which, luckily, were of the clip-on type since neither Deirdre nor I had pierced ears. Topping off this glamorous outfit, a deep-pink rosebud was pinned above my left bosom.

My father drove us to Aylward Hall and we were escorted from our car by handsome Charlie, wearing Dad's tuxedo that had been taken out of mothballs for this auspicious occasion. He also sported striped trousers and black patent-leather shoes.

On negotiating the marble staircase in the great hall, our best friend, Bella, descended upon us.

"How simply gorgeous you both look," she cooed. She herself was a symphony in blue organza, the bodice tight and low-cut, the skirt in many layers of satin ribbon and lace falling away from the tiny waist.

A hint of envy crept in here for we knew Bella had spent many hours closeted at the ladies' wear shop, *Á La Mode*, in the High Street. The dress had been specially designed for her and fitted to perfection. My white sheath did feel slightly cumbersome in comparison, but I consoled myself with the fact that her dress was so – well, so *French*, and after all, this was a very British occasion.

A waiter hovered nearby with a silver tray bearing an assortment of colourful glasses.

"Dubonnet, Modom?" queried the waiter, proffering his tray.

"I don't mind if I do," I said, grabbing a tall glass with a cherry sticking out of the top. Deirdre took a small glass containing something dark and boring.

"Modom has selected a Tom Collins," corrected the waiter. "Your sister took the Dubonnet."

Having dispensed this vital information he swept away, pirouetting like a circus performer, and without spilling a drop, deftly offered the tray to some other guests trailing up the white stairs.

We sauntered around, trying to lose Charlie, who, for some inexplicable reason suddenly seemed devoted to his twin sisters. After mingling and saying hello to everyone and admiring all the gowns, we were separated. I stopped to examine the array of delectable food on the long tables. I recognized miniature sausage rolls and shrimp canapés, but was mystified by some tiny crinkle-edged pies. The waitress kindly told me they were *chicken bouchées*. There were dainty sandwiches and wafer-thin ham wrapped round asparagus; mysterious things on sticks and some black stuff, which looked like ball-bearings. I would look at the menu later to find this was caviar. I didn't fancy it though, however fascinating it seemed.

I decided I would fill up on the trifle for dessert; it was sitting aside in an enormous glass bowl.

Bella caught up with me. "You must try the *paté de foie gras*. It's simply divine."

"What's this?" I asked, pointing to slivers of meat, which appeared to be falling out of puff pastry.

"Oh, darling, they're the *roasted grouse vol-au-vents*," said Bella, stuffing a whole one in her mouth to prove how tasty they were. I had to tell her she had flaky pastry all down the front of her blue organza. She rushed to the powder room.

I bumped into Deirdre who seemed to be eating cucumber out of a glass. She waved a sprig of mint at me and then put a slice of lemon in her mouth. "This was a Pimm's No. 1 – simply smashing – it practically had a whole salad in it."

My stiletto heels were making me wobbly so I found a convenient step at the top of the stairs and sank down.

"Oooh, I didn't get one of those," I exclaimed, as the waiter waltzed by with a solitary elegant pink glass triangle on his tray.

"Pink Gin," said the waiter, almost tipping the lone glass into my lap.

I discarded the shoes and was just struggling to my feet, having to hitch up my dress to do so, when a strong hand grasped mine and I was pulled up. It was Bella's brother, Nigel. I smiled my thanks for his assistance, while he immediately turned to the wall and said, "Angela! Remember? I wanted to show you this marvelous painting that my uncle sent from Italy."

To my horror something fell into my half empty glass. It was my left diamanté earring. I was terrified I would have to swallow this while I finished the drink, but luckily Nigel was so immersed in his uncle's painting he did not notice my fingers retrieve the piece of jewellery and return it, dripping, to my ear.

Whilst Nigel was regaling me with the sheer artistry of the horrible daub of colour from his uncle, he never took his eyes off it. I knew he was keen on modern art, but there is no accounting for some people's taste. It was quite shocking.

I tried to slip my shoes back on and then I noticed a red streak down the front of my white dress. It was time to go.

"Is that Dubonnet or Pink Gin?" giggled Deirdre.

Something else was amiss. My deep-pink rosebud had disappeared. All that remained was a bit of wilted green stem held by a safety pin above my left bosom. I was also tripping over the front hem of my dress, which had come undone.

We headed towards the stairs where Charlie was waiting for us.

"I don't think we were supposed to stay the full two hours," said Deirdre, looking at her watch.

I noticed most of the guests had disappeared. We left, properly murmuring our thanks and goodbyes.

Once more, I tried to put my shoes on. "This was my first cocktail party," I announced proudly, to no one in particular.

"It will be your last if Mom sees you like this," promised Charlie, opening the car door.

"Hello, Henry. Straight home!" I said to the chauffeur, who also happened to be our much older brother. He had purposely missed the party as he said it was only for kids, like us.

Well, it didn't really matter. We now knew all about cocktail parties, and obviously, it was fatal to stay too long. Next time we would do better. We had lots of time to perfect this art. We hoped the real thing would be just as much fun as this make-believe one. But we would have to wait a few years. Deirdre and I were only twelve years old.

THE REUNION

"Is it really fifteen years since we left school?" Donna plonked her suitcase onto one of the queen size beds. No one said anything. The other three knew it was not really a question – more of a statement, made to no one in particular, but to everyone generally. School principals speak that way, and Donna had been one for several years.

"How come we're sharing a room?" asked Sarah, the lawyer, kicking off her shoes and flopping onto the other bed.

"Well, I know you've been divorced for three years and not used to sharing with anyone, but I thought it would be more fun this way," said Jenny, the farmer's wife, placing her suitcase on the rack by the door. "We always used to share – in the old days."

"Yes, but that was when we had no money," said Leanne, the Corporate Queen. "We don't have to worry about that now."

Speak for yourself, thought Jenny who had had to scrimp and save up cash for the hotel and for the airfare from

Alberta. She carefully took the borrowed dress out of the case and hung it up.

"Well, I don't mind sharing a bed with you, Leanne, so long as you don't still have your nightmares and suddenly start yelling and kicking in the middle of the night," said Donna. Then, on seeing Jenny's dress, she asked, "Is that for tonight? A bit over the top, isn't it?"

For a farmer's wife, Donna could have added. Jenny winced. Donna, always the conservative, modest school teacher, now on her pedestal as a principal. Yes, a school principal might think that the dress was over the top. "Isn't it what you'd wear for a Gala Reunion Dinner?" Jenny defended herself. She had been looking forward to wearing this stunning dress.

"Yeah, just kidding," said Donna, getting hers out. Modest, simple styling, but well cut, pale grey, exactly what a school principal might wear.

"Well, I brought three, 'cos I couldn't make up my mind," said Leanne. "You girls will have to help me decide." She proceeded to take her dresses out and hang them next to Jenny's long, shimmering navy gown.

"Black short, black long, and black two piece," laughed Sarah. "Same as ever: the blonde in black. Wait till you see mine. I haven't worn hot pink for years. Maybe you should wear the hot pink, Leanne, as you're getting this year's Alumni award. Hey, girls, aren't we going to have a drink? Where's the gin and tonic?"

Jenny plonked the bottle of gin on the table. She poured the drinks, carefully measuring out the gin, adding the tonic, inserting a twist of lemon.

"Oh, not for me, thanks," said Leanne. "I've got to look through my speech. I'll go out on the balcony; I need a cigarette." She gathered up her lighter, cigarettes, and a bright green binder which displayed the name *Zuyder-Zurich Laboratories Inc.* and slid open the balcony door.

"My Ex has shares in that company," said Sarah, taking the glass Jenny offered her.

"So has everyone else," said Donna.

Everybody except me, thought Jenny.

The dinner went well. Leanne graciously accepted her award – a metallic statue, which, at a casual glance, looked a bit like an Oscar. She, in turn, presented some prizes to the students of the Vancouver Island Academy for Girls.

Her speech was so good – full of humorous stories of her rise to CEO of Zuyder/Zurich Pharmaceuticals, peppered with tales of her international travels and an explanation of why she hardly ever came back to Canada. A very short explanation, actually, which was a villa on the edge of a lake in Switzerland.

Sarah was asked to make a short speech as well, about her work in the legal profession. She, too, handed out a few awards to students.

Donna was also acknowledged – hadn't she done well to become principal of Gordon Bennett School in Prince George?

And then, what of Jenny, the farmer's wife from the rich pastures of Alberta, where, as well as helping her husband raise cattle, she was also fully occupied raising four children? No mention was made of her at the Gala Reunion Dinner.

"Always thought you were going to be a nurse, Jenny," said Leanne as they drove back to the hotel.

"So I was,' said Jenny with a rueful smile, "but, as you all know, before I qualified I got pregnant, got married, and gave up nurses' training, in that order."

"And then you were too busy having three more babies to go back to nursing," said Sarah, whose career in motherhood had been submerged by that of a lawyer. She had allowed her ex-husband custody of their two children, a matter that could easily be reversed, whenever she had the inkling. But she hadn't – not yet.

Donna's only child was at boarding school in Ontario, to be near the grandparents. Her husband had died only five years after they were married. Her school was her family now.

As for Leanne, she had never married. She had been too busy climbing the corporate ladder. Successful Leanne. She had one vice, though. She smoked a pack a day. As soon as she got back to the hotel, she grabbed her Players and headed out the balcony door, alone.

"You'd think she would have given it up by now," said Sarah. "Working for a pharmaceuticals company and all."

"Just like you've given up the booze," said Donna with a wink at Jenny.

The cards were dealt and the wine poured, and soon it was almost midnight.

"We don't have to check out till noon tomorrow," said Leanne, coming back into the room after another smoke, "so let's all have a nightcap of that gin while we have another hand of cards. I haven't won yet. I've got to beat the farmer's wife."

The level of gin went down and the laughter increased. Squealing with amusement, Leanne threw down her cards and took off the top part of her outfit. "Lost my shirt. Knew I would someday."

"Wouldn't it be fun if we could all swap lives for a while," said Sarah. "I'd be a dab hand at farming."

"Come off it, Sarah. You wouldn't know a cow from a steer," said Leanne.

"Well, I'd like to see how you got along milking a cow — or a steer."

"We don't have any dairy cows," said Jenny. "We raise only beef cattle."

"Well, that's even easier," said Leanne. "No milking. You could stay in bed till eight every morning."

Her speech was getting slurred. "Going for another puff – didn't finish that other one." She made for the balcony door.

"You'd better put your top on," said the ever-cautionary Donna. "And close that door, *s'il vous plait*; it's windy out there and we don't want your downdraft."

It was Donna who noticed that Leanne had been gone longer than usual. "What's keeping her?" She opened the balcony door and hollered so loud they all jumped up and ran outside. Leanne was slumped over the table.

"She's dead," screamed Sarah.

"No, she's not," said Jenny feeling Leanne's pulse. "Sarah, help me get her on the floor. Donna, grab a blanket. And call an ambulance"

With expertise that surprised the other two, Jenny performed CPR on Leanne, whose eyelids flickered and opened. "What happened?" she croaked.

"Your heart ... I think," said Jenny, standing up.

"How d'you know?" asked Sarah.

"I've kept up my First Aid," said Jenny. "And don't forget, I **was** going to be a nurse."

"You still could be," said Donna. "You **should** be."

The ambulance arrived.

"Yes, it's probably her heart," said one of the paramedics fielding the girls' questions, as Leanne was strapped to a gurney. "We'll get her to hospital. You did well for your friend," he said to Jenny. "Probably saved her life."

Yes, it had been **some** Reunion.

THE PLAN

The Plan was to get Lars away from Maria. He had been mooning after her for months, ever since he went to her eighteenth birthday party. He had been invited only because he happened to be a friend of Maria's brother, Tony.

Her best friend, Shannon, knew Maria was likewise besotted with Lars. She had to admit he was very handsome, so blond, and so ... Scandinavian.

"She's my little sister, for crying out loud," said Tony. He couldn't see for the life of him why Lars was so entranced with Maria. "There are better looking girls at the tennis club."

Maria was the first girl Lars had fallen for in a romantic, sexless way. He thought it must be pure love. Tony thought it was pure nonsense.

And Maria's father had told her straight off the bat that he wouldn't have his daughter seeing that fair-haired layabout with his Danish name and manners. Maria had even accused her father of racism. Well, wasn't that what it amounted to? Her father going on about fair, Danish looks versus dark, Italian looks.

"Who does he think he is anyway? A second Hans Christian Anderson? He certainly has the Gift of the Gab."

This was after seeing samples of Lars's stories and poems in the local paper. Mr. Marconi might have approved of an Italian boyfriend, no doubt, but not right now. He laid down the law; his daughter was to get to University and Romance was definitely not on the agenda at this time.

It had been like the Cyber Spy Agency. Her father wasn't called Marconi for nothing. He knew a lot about electronics. Suddenly, her cell-phone service was blocked and the lovers had to resort to hand-written love letters, which Shannon had carried back and forth surreptitiously. Daddy Marconi soon cottoned on to this and forbade Maria to receive such notes. But Lars was so insistent and love-torn, how could Shannon refuse to deliver a few more?

There were a few variations to the Plan. First, Tony had what he thought was a brilliant idea to tell his sister that Lars was after another girl. Well, obviously, Tony knew nothing of psychology. That would make Maria want him all the more. Shannon had the idea to tell her that Lars wasn't eating and was wasting away. That would put Maria off, for sure.

"That's ridiculous,' said Tony. "Everyone knows boys don't get anorexia. That won't work."

However, Shannon had begun to notice that the novelty of amorous letters was becoming irksome to Maria. She was succumbing to parental pressure. Maybe she had seen the Writing on the Wall.

Yes, the Plan was going to work, Shannon could see that. And, added to this, Maria seemed to be concentrating on her studies to get into University in Montreal. She was going to be a doctor, just like her cousin, Rugiero. The family was very proud of **him**.

Lars was angry when Shannon told him that Maria had trashed a note from him, unopened. "Don't shoot the messenger," she said.

She also told him, "I'm not delivering any more letters. Maria doesn't want them, anyway".

The Plan was working. Mr. Marconi's mantra was obviously *out of sight – out of mind*. Trips to the cabin had been curtailed and the skiing trip cancelled, to make sure there was no danger of her bumping into Lars whose family also frequented those places. This was all in the name of education. She had to pass that exam.

She **did** pass the exam. Shannon's best friend, Maria, went to medical school in Montreal, to start her chosen profession. The Plan had worked.

And Shannon would be a nurse, but a lovesick one at that.

The Plan had somehow back-fired.

Yes, she was hopelessly in love with Lars herself.

A ONE PAGE PIECE

My readers have told me they are tired of my long stories, sometimes five or more pages. My New Year's resolution is to give them a one page piece.

They are quite right. Long stories are a trial to the reader. They should be banned.

Many writers, famous and otherwise have been guilty of such offences. Look at Earnest Hemingway, for instance. He wrote all those books with enigmatic characters who talk themselves off the page. If all that dialogue was cut, the book would be a manageable length.

Tolstoy is another prime example. In *War and Peace* if he had missed out some of the war and all the love scenes, we would just have a bit of peace left. I mean, it took the BBC ten episodes to portray this epic on TV. It would have saved them a lot of trouble if Tolstoy had not got carried away.

And look at Shakespeare. Instead of going on about "the moon, the inconstant moon that monthly changes in her circled orb ...." which takes up two pages, he could just have said, "The moon was out, and so was Juliet, and Romeo fell for her." Because their parents hated each other, Romeo and Juliet cooked up a pretty complex way of carrying on their love affair. She pretended to kill herself by poison. Romeo thought she was really dead, so, wishing to join her, **he** drank some poison. Juliet woke up and finding Romeo now a corpse, eventually finishes herself off with his dagger. It's just your everyday story of gangs and drugs. Shakespeare could have saved a lot of paper and ink.

Then there's the Bible; an enormous book. Whether in the St. James' version with all those "thee's, thou's, and hath's," or the modern version which is only slightly shorter, churchgoers only have time to read a few verses each Sunday. Take Abraham, Moses and Isaiah in the Old Testament, and you've got most of the famous people. In the New Testament, there was Jesus who was born the Son of God and lots of people say he was not the Son of God at all and it is all a fairy tale. Oh, in the Old Testament, I missed out Joseph who was an early victim of bullying because of his brightly coloured hoodie. That makes a good story and should not be cut out since Joseph does a lot better than his bullying brothers. He goes to Egypt where he gets friendly with the Pharaoh and gives out advice. Nowadays he would be called the Prime Minister of Egypt but even back then, nobody liked Egyptian politics. Yes, the Bible is definitely too long.

Charles Dickens was a master story teller, but it is an endurance test having to wade through his multi-page descriptions of Victorian London. Whether it's *Oliver Twist* or *Little Dorrit*, once having described their haunts, Dickens could have just put a footnote – *Ibid* – in all further novels, to save space and eye-strain for the reader. It's a pity he didn't have the advantage of what most people use now: text language. You don't need much space for that.

On the other hand, unlike the above-mentioned Shakespearean lovers, Rhett Butler and Scarlet O'Hara in *Gone with the Wind* don't seem to be quite sure whether they want each other or not. You have to sift through details of the Civil War to find out what Margaret Mitchell had in mind, and then she leaves you guessing in the end, which hardly seems fair after all that reading.

Oh, I'm so sorry; I have just realized I have exceeded one page. I could possibly rectify this by using a smaller font.

Finally, it occurred to me that one way to save space is to pepper the text with Latin phrases. They are much shorter than regular English ones. *Dictum Factum* (No sooner said than done).

THAT'S WHAT FRIENDS ARE FOR

"There's something I need to tell you," I said to Lara, as we left the office.

"Is that why we're going for coffee without the others?" she asked. "It must be something important."

"It's about your husband."

"What about him?"

"He's having an affair." There was no way to beat about the bush, I thought, speaking in hushed tones even though there was no one else within earshot.

"For goodness sake, Cindy, give me some credit," said Lara. "You think I didn't know?"

I was taken aback. "Well, aren't you upset?"

"Upset? What's there to get upset about? This has been going on since our third wedding anniversary, when I found out not all his dentist appointments were for real. That dental hygienist worked some weird hours, I must say."

I was dumbfounded. Lara didn't seem to care.

"Hell, no. I'm not upset. I have my own ... compensations," she said.

"Then you really don't mind?" This was much easier than I had thought.

"No, it doesn't bother me. The only thing is, I'd love to know who the latest bitch is so I can tell her she's welcome to him."

"You're looking right at her," I said.

Lara didn't bat an eyelid. "There's something I need to tell you, too. It's about **your** husband."

ANN GIJSBERS

OF ANGELS AND FAIRIES

"Do you believe in angels and fairies?" Melanie asked her best friend, Anna.

"No I don't. Do you?"

"I guess." Melanie shrugged her shoulders. "My Mom always reads me stories about them before I go to bed, and that makes me dream. But I don't know the difference between them. They both have wings, don't they?"

"Why do you ask me? I've never seen one."

It was a warm, late September afternoon, such as only an Indian summer can bring forth. The girls, both second grade students, were walking home from their country school, but, even in the short distance they had to go, the sweltering air had slowed them down. It was a good time to loaf around and so they perched themselves on the log fence of a neighbour's farm for a rest. Swinging her legs while humming a tune, Melanie forgot about her question and suddenly cried out in delight.

"Look at all the blue Chicory flowers! They always bloom around my birthday. Maybe that's why they are my favourite colour. And my Mom's too. I'll go and pick some for her."

She slid down to the ground and since there were so many, she soon had a pretty bouquet. Happily she showed it to her friend.

"Do they smell nice?" Anna asked.

"Not really, but look at all the petals each flower has. Take a guess how many."

Anna's eyebrows pulled together in a frown.

"Why do you ask me all these things? It's too warm to think." Then she smiled when an idea popped up in her mind.

"You could count them while you pull them apart, like you do with daisies. Then do... you know... *he loves me, he loves me not.*"

"No way," Melanie interrupted her friend. "I don't like all that mushy stuff."

"Well," said Anna. "You can say something else like, *fairies are real, fairies are not.* Then you would know about the angels and fairies too."

Melanie bent to put her bouquet on the grass, picked one more flower, and hoisted herself back up on the fence. While carefully detaching each flower from its anchor, her little voice chanted, "they are, they are not, they are, they are not."

"Oh no. I pulled two at the same time. Now what?"

"Nothing," Anna said, "It'll stay a mystery. But I'm going home. I'm thirsty. Maybe my Mom made lemonade."

The idea of a cool drink was enticing to Melanie too, and slowly the girls strolled along the country lane. Lazy bumble bees swarmed around and crickets jumped out of the way, but the birds were too warm to sing. Then, suddenly, out of a duckweed covered ditch, a big frog jumped up and started to croak loudly.

"Wow, see that?" Anna exclaimed. "I've never seen one that big."

Melanie stopped and pondered. "Maybe it's a Prince in disguise. Want to go and kiss him?"

"Yugh," Anna giggled. "Anyway, I'm not a Princess."

"But we could pretend."

"You kiss him, then," and Anna started to run away.

Catching up with her, Melanie panted, "I still like to believe he's a Prince. Don't you think that is exciting?"

By now the girls had reached Anna's home and parted. Waving goodbye to her friend, Anna joked, "See you tomorrow, Princess. Are you going to wear your crown?"

"No. My wings," Melanie laughed. "I'd rather be a fairy."

She walked a little further down the road and then skipped the gravelled driveway to the back door of home. There she was happily surprised to find her grandmother opening it. With a big hug, she handed her the pretty flowers, as if she had gathered them especially for her.

"Oh thank you darling. Gee, if you are not my sweet little angel."

Angel? Melanie thought, *Did an angel make her do this?*

Angels and Fairies. Somehow they always popped up, so there must be some truth in all the stories about them. You just have to believe in their magic. Then she smiled, feeling content with her own conclusion.

TURKEY TIME

Miss Bell was discussing the meaning of Thanksgiving Day with her Grade 2 students. Explaining the origin of it in her usual colorful way, she drew a vivid imaginable picture of the journey done by a hundred and two pilgrims, about four hundred years ago. How they had left their homeland, England, by boat, to find a place where they could live in peace. A place where they could live according to the religion they had chosen, but for which they were hunted in their native country.

It had been a very difficult and tiresome sailing. Boats in those days were no modern cruise ships. The Mayflower, in which they came, was not even built for passengers but as a cargo ship. It must have been terrible on stormy days, when the waves were enormously high, to be tossed around in the ship's hull.

After a month at sea, they finally reached the shore of the New Land, America. But here, another challenge was waiting. There was neither shelter nor food for them, so with the limited supplies they had brought with them, they started to build a log house and planted a garden. That, too, was not as easy as it would be today, because there were no power tools. Everything had to be done manually, which required lots of hard labour. But they made a good start and, in the meantime, became friends with some neighbouring native Indians. This proved to be their salvation later, for the first winter in their newly established colony was a very bad one. Snow and ice made life almost unbearable and they ran out of food as well. Half of the pilgrims died and it was only through the graceful help of the natives that the others survived.

Throughout the following spring and summer they worked hard again and succeeded in growing so much food that, by Fall, there was a good supply for the coming winter. They were so grateful, that they dedicated a special day to give thanks to the Lord for blessing their efforts. A special meal was prepared from the bountiful harvest and shared with the friendly natives. This became a tradition and even now we celebrate Thanksgiving Day, taking time to think about all the good things we enjoy.

Here Miss Bell paused, searching the faces of the children in front of her. Could they relate to her story at all and understand the overwhelming gratitude those people felt so many years ago? How corn and turkey had been such a feast?

She checked her watch. Almost time for the bell to ring, meaning school was finished for today and the long weekend would begin. On a sudden impulse she asked her students to think about her story while celebrating and search their own mind what to be thankful for.

Four days later, back in the classroom, she asked the children about their thoughts during the holiday. There were plenty of answers dealing with food, family and home. But, Miss Bell pointed out, although those are the most important things in life, they should be counted as blessings every day. At Thanksgiving, it was time for something very special. Did any of her students have an idea?

The first one to raise his hand was Benny.

"I was thankful that I could see all the beautiful coloured trees, and later, when we had raked the fallen leaves in a pile, we had fun kicking around in them. You can't do that in the spring."

Jake was next. "I went fishing with my Dad and we got a big one. Mom stuffed it and it went on the barbeque. It tasted even better than turkey. But, it was our last outdoor meal for this year and all of us were thankful that the weather was still sunny and warm."

Cindy told the class, "I helped my Dad to pick up a lot of fallen apples in our yard and we brought them to the food bank. Did the natives grow apples and did they bring them to the pilgrims too? Could they make apple pie? My Mom always does and I love them."

Another answer came from Robin. "Is it true that the natives were the first ones to grow corn? Who told them how to do it? And where did they get the seeds? My Dad orders it from the seed catalogue but I don't think they had catalogues back then. I am very grateful that those Indians invented it though, 'cause they are my favourite veggie." Then, as an afterthought, he added, "With butter!"

Miss Bell smiled, pleased with the answers, even though most of them were related to food anyway. "I have time for one more. How about you Ashley?"

Ashley's happy face suddenly wrinkled up in thoughts, contemplating a clever answer. Finally she said, "I was just thankful that I'm not a turkey."

WAVES

I first noticed the girl when she entered the departure waiting room of the Georgia Straight ferry. Dressed in loose layers of earth-toned garments, dusty brown, dull green and faded tan, wearing hiking boots which showed signs of having conquered many an outdoor trail, she came across as a free-spirited wanderer.

Unloading the heavy backpack from her shoulders, she sat down near a window, opened a bag and rummaged through it. Out came a hunk of bread, a glass jar with undisclosed contents and a crooked metallic spoon. Soon she was enjoying a seemingly tasty breakfast.

I lost track of her during the ferry crossing but her image stayed in my mind. Strangely enough, I found myself comparing her with the waves gliding past the boat. I always thought the white caps were riding along on top of the waves. However on close observation I noticed the foam crests to the top and then, instead of moving along, falls back and meets the next wave. Aimless. Just drifting. Looking for new adventure.

I forgot about the girl until I took my place on a bus which would bring me from the harbour into the big city of Vancouver.

She came in, too, and sat across from me, her heavy boots firmly planted on the floor, bulging backpack beside her. Then, draping the wide skirt over her knees, she parted her legs, thus making a basket in her lap. Now out of a bag came some badly tangled balls and hanks of macramé. Dropping them into her improvised holder, she moved her knees a little closer together to prevent the material rolling on the floor by every curve of the swaying bus. She fascinated me and while trying not to appear too inquisitive, I watched her closely.

Moving on to the task of unravelling and keeping the different colours apart, her young hands worked steadily, twisting skinny strands together making sure they were all of the same length. "For what, all this effort?" I wondered. "To weave into her hair?"

Seeing her sitting there, I could not help but think how vulnerable she looked. In contrast to her dirty fingernails, her face was clean, almost naïve, in an old fashioned way. Pure. Without makeup. Her cheeks soft and rosy, she could have passed for a peasant girl from decades ago.

While her fingers kept going, she looked up at a man sitting nearby and asked for directions as they approached the city centre. He replied very kindly and soon they were engaged in a lively conversation.

He looked twice her age and although far better dressed, his luggage had the same appearance as that of the girl. Only, he had twice as much and, if possible, his load was even bulkier. Their talk was mainly about places they'd like to go to and where each had been.

Immense pleasure radiated from their faces as if they had been long-lost friends. Though slightly reserved and almost dignified, the girl spoke without hesitation, inspired by the man's enthusiasm.

By the time the desired bus stop was reached they got off together, hauling their bags behind them and, while the bus waited for the traffic light to turn green, I watched her go. Walking with strong strides in those sturdy boots, each step she took slightly lifted her skirt and revealed thick home-knitted socks. The man, light-footed in runners, moved ahead of her, guiding her through the oncoming crowd. To where? Like whitecaps on a wave? Drifting, always restless, until maybe one day they'd reach a shore?

Once in a while, the girl comes across my mind again and, in my heart, I wish her a safe journey.

TRICK OR TREAT?

"Mom, do we really have to go to Annaville now? I'll miss all the Hallowe'en fun."

Sitting in the car's back seat, behind the driver, Jacky was questioning her Mom's decision to go there today.

"Hon, I explained it to you yesterday, but I'll go over it again. After Grandma passed away, Grandpa moved into a retirement home. Now their house is up for sale, but it has to be emptied first. That's a big job and I'm so glad Uncle Bert will be able to help me, but since this is strictly the only time he can come, we have no choice but to go there now," Holly answered.

"Will Cathy and Carl be there too?"

"No Jacky, the twins stayed home with their mother. I'm sure they would have loved to come; we hardly get to see each other. But, flying all the way across Canada costs a lot of money, and driving that distance takes too long. Besides, the kids have to go to school."

"Well, then, how come I don't have to? I could have stayed with Auntie Jennifer."

"Yes, I'm sure that would have been nice, but Jennifer had to work nightshift and could not change it on short notice."

Holly looked at her daughter in the rear-view mirror and saw a serious little face.

"She's not my real aunt, is she Mom?"

"No, hon, she's not a blood relation, but she could not be any closer with her heart."

"Ugh, Mom. Blood sounds creepy. It makes me think of Halloween monsters. But I'd like to go trick or treating anyway. Maybe at Grannies neighbours? Did you bring my costume?"

"Oh gosh! I forgot! We were in such a hurry. Yes, I think you can go. You can join the kids next door. You know them all. But I don't know what to do about a costume for you"

Taking the village exit off the freeway, Holly thought of how much she would miss her parents' home. She had had such wonderful years there, growing up in a loving atmosphere. However, Mom had passed away this summer and since Dad was so much older, there was no other option for him than to go into an adult care home.

At first she had contemplated moving back here with him, but she knew she would never find a job as good as the one she had now, in the town where she had started a new life. This job secured fulfilment of her dearest wish as a single parent, to be able to raise her daughter happily and safely. Even her brother, Bert, had advised her by phone not to change. So she was greatly relieved when Dad had settled quite well in his new home, making friends with other residents who helped to fill the empty space in his heart. He sure missed his caring wife.

"Mom! You passed Grandma's house," Jacky yelled from the back seat.

"Wow! So I did!" Holly woke up from her thoughts and eased the car backward. By the time she had reached the driveway, the front door had opened already and Bert was running up to meet them.

"Hi Sis," he welcomed her. "Glad to see you! This house is lonely without the old folks in it."

"Glad to see you, too," Holly hugged her brother.

"Me too!" came a little voice from inside the car and Bert hastened to scoop Jacky into his arms.

Once inside, Holly looked around. Nothing had changed yet. Still, Bert was right, there was a different feeling all around. The coziness was gone.

"Let's put the kettle on," she said. "I could use a cup of tea. And what about supper? When was your last meal Bert?"

He grinned, "Breakfast."

"Poor you! Jacky, could you find the biscuits in that box with food I brought? They will have to do till I get organised."

Bert's gaze followed his little niece while she skipped across the room.

"You sure have grown tall since I saw you last. Does your mother feed you broomsticks?" he joked.

"Broomsticks are for witches, Uncle Bert, and I don't want to be a witch." Then, suddenly remembering, Jacky added, "I could not even be one if I wanted to, I have no costume whatsoever for tomorrow." Facing her mother with a question in her eyes she pleaded hopefully, "Or ... can we ...?"

A knock on the door interrupted her and she jumped up to be surprised by her holiday friends from down the street. It was a happy, noisy reunion, one child talking even more excitedly than the other. But even through the commotion some organising came forth. Jacky could get dressed up for Hallowe'en after all because Uncle Bert offered to take her to Annaville to buy a costume. Then, in the meantime, Holly could unpack the suitcases and make dinner.

It was only a twenty–minute drive to town, for which Bert was grateful. He had travelled enough that day and airports were no fun. However Jacky's happy face made it worthwhile and he realised how lucky his own children were to have both a father and a mother. If only Holly lived closer, then he could do more for his niece, too. But a well-paying, secure job was most important right now, and they always kept in close contact by computer and phone.

The busy department store was still well stocked for the last days of October and Jacky had no problem finding a Tinkerbell costume. She danced excitedly through the store, new treasure in her arms. However, not looking where she was going, she bumped into a glass display case. It crashed down, flooring her and slashing her right arm. Bewildered she stared at it.

"Uncle Bert, look at it. I hate blood."

True enough, red trails were running out of the wound. Bert tried to stop it with a clean handkerchief but to no avail. There was no way of stopping the flow. Store clerks came running and waived his offer to compensate for the mess, saying he'd better take his niece to the hospital only two blocks away.

Sitting in the car, she held tight to an improvised bandage while also clutching her new outfit under her other arm. Smiling bravely to her Uncle, she announced, "It doesn't even hurt."

Bert realized then that it was a deep cut. The throbbing pain would come later.

They were lucky at the emergency ward, no long line-up and Jacky was looked after in a caring friendly manner. It was a serious wound, however, so stitches were required, which made them late coming home. Of course, there was a lot to explain, but, after the excitement died down, the hunger pangs took over.

"Mmmm...mmm!" Bert said. "There's nothing that makes a house a home like the smell of a good meal being cooked."

"Yes", Holly thought, "it already feels more like the old house we used to know. If only we can sleep well too. We'll need it."

Lucky enough, the next morning both brother and sister woke up with plenty of energy to start a difficult task of cleaning up and evaluating all that was left behind. Dad had taken along what he had wanted to keep, so that was one less worry. Jacky's arm, however, was very painful and to help her cope with it Holly suggested that she could go up to the attic and see if the trunk with old toys was still there. Meanwhile, the adults started to divide keepsakes from garage-sale items. Still, some decisions were hard to make and time flew by. Even for Jacky who had fun with old toys and clothes.

"I could have dressed up in some of these," she said pointing to the pile of outdated garments. "Uncle Bert, was this your soccer uniform?"

"Well, what do you know? Yes, it is! Did Mom ever throw anything away? I think you should stick to your Tinkerbell outfit though; it'll look prettier on you. Don't you agree Holly?"

"You're right. So get dressed Jacky, your friends next door might be waiting for you already."

Soon the air outside filled with laughter and ghost cries, while scary and pretty little creatures alike demanded their treats. Then, after quite a while, everything quieted down again when all the goblins, creepy monsters and fairies, including Jacky, returned home.

She happily spread all her goodies on the table, sharing some with the grownups. But, alas, Tinkerbell's magic would come to an end. Bedtime was long past and Holly took her daughter upstairs to tuck her in.

Back in the living room, Holly could not help but vocalise her thoughts.

"I'm glad that's over again."

"Why?" Bert wanted to know.

"Just memories."

"True. Some are melancholic. Look at me," Bert laughed, holding his soccer shorts in front of him. "I loved that game and the fun we used to have. Life was easy, then." Looking down at himself, he added, "Couldn't fit into these things anymore."

Just then, there was a loud bang on the door. Holly looked at her brother, puzzled.

"It's a little late for more goblins and ghosts. Do you mind answering it Bert?"

Complying with her request, he looked puzzled himself when he did find a tall ghost standing before him. Out of that white mass a voice protruded with a question.

"Is this the Dober residence?"

"It is, or rather, it was," a stunned Bert replied. "But who are you? Somehow your voice seems familiar."

"I hadn't expected you here," the voice continued, "but since you are, maybe you can help me. May I come in for a minute?"

Bert turned around to look at his sister and was shocked by her ashen face.

"Holly?"

Unable to answer right away, Holly's mind had raced back to another Hallowe'en and the echo of a voice she'd heard that night came back to her. That voice had whispered so many sweet words to her then, yet after that evening, she had never heard it again. It had belonged to her brother's best friend, a boy two years older than she was. She had always adored him but it was not until she had finished high school that he had taken more notice of her. Their friendship had blossomed and soon it had become more than that. He had come home from university that time to celebrate Halloween with her and after the party, he had walked her home.

Passing the graveyard, she had confessed to him that she was very scared of ghosts and was almost shaking. He had held her close then, comforting her in the misty darkness. It had felt so good. Too good, maybe?

"Holly?" Bert's voice broke the spell. "This man or I presume that's what is inside this ghost costume, would like to see Mom and Dad."

Facing the creature again, Bert asked, "What is your reason for this call? Are you from a real estate group? The house will be up for sale, but we are not ready, yet. Why are you dressed like that, anyway?"

"I'd like to keep my identity hidden until I have some information. Depending on that, I'll stay or go."

Still very nervous, but partly recovered from the shock, Holly joined the conversation.

"I think I know this ghost Bert, and so do you. If I'm correct this is your old friend, Jacques Roland."

"Well, I'll be..." Bert yanked at his friend's disguise. "I knew the voice, but I couldn't place it right away. Come on in. Okay Holly?"

His sister shrugged her shoulders. "I guess."

They sat down and while Bert fired a hundred questions, Jacques and Holly stole a few awkward glances at each other.

"So, did you come to buy the house?" Bert wanted to know.

"No, I really came to find an answer to a long burning question. Please let me explain. Yesterday in the hospital emergency where I work now as an intern, I saw a little girl who made my mind go into orbit. She was a young but precise replica of a girl I loved dearly, one who never left my dreams. I simply had to find out who that girl was but I was called away.

Jacky Dober was her name. The girl I loved went by the name of Holly Dober. Coincidence? I'm here to find out."

"I see, but why now?" Holly could not think of anything else to say. "Six years ago you vanished like a ship in the Bermuda Triangle, without a trace of any kind."

"Not so. I wrote you a long letter of explanation, which was far harder to do than any of my exams. To wait for your answer almost killed me but after a few months I realised that you must have had second thoughts about the two of us, and I dove into my studies to forget the pain."

"But I never did get a letter from you."

"Bert?" Jacques now turned his attention to his old school buddy. "I gave it to you to make sure your sister would get it. It was during our last soccer match together. How I hated to go. I never did tell you I had to leave or why."

Bert looked sheepish. He slightly remembered that day, but after their win they all went out for a beer and, come to think of it, he did have a few too many drinks that time. Later, he often wondered where in the world Jacques had gone, but finally, after inquiring at the Dean's office, he learned that his friend had transferred to a university in Quebec.

Now he got up and felt inside the soccer shorts pockets, producing a greyish crumpled envelope.

"Impossible to decipher," he said. "It must have gone through the washer and I never played again after you were gone, Jacques."

Taking courage from the fact that Holly wasn't wearing a wedding band, Jacques, looking tenderly at her, started to reveal what message the letter held.

"Holly, that Halloween evening I realised that our love was taking complete charge of our lives. I also knew that I badly wanted to become a physician and that I could not throw two years of study away. If I stayed close to you I would get impatient, want to get married, have children. Yet we were still so young. I had no choice but to move away, study hard, and come back for you when I had my degree.

"I begged you to wait for me and write that you would. We could keep close by mail. But the answer never came. Maybe you had found out about my secret? In order to pay for my studies in which my parents could not support me, I had started to deal in drugs. I didn't want to have a huge debt by the time I was finished. I was lucky, never got caught, although my conscience still bothers me about it. I try to make up for it now by being a good and caring doctor and I was very lucky to get appointed to Annaville. It felt good to be home again. But, here the dream of the one and only love in my life came haunting back, too. I was drawn to the house where she lived, but there was no one there and the neighbours told me that everybody had moved. Yet, there was this little girl yesterday. Jacky Dober. Same name, same address."

"Yes, I'm Jacky Dober." A small, nightgown –clad figure entered the room.

"Mom, I can't sleep, my arm bothers me. Can I have some more candy?"

Jacques looked at her with admiration. With a question in his eyes, he looked at Holly who spoke shyly, "Meet your daughter Jacques. Yes, your very own daughter.   . That's why her name is Jacky." Then, with a soft smile on her face, Holly added, "Even though I had a lot of help from my parents, she was my only sunbeam during very sad and difficult times."

"Now I'd like to have a word, too." Bert got to his feet. "I'm absolutely flabbergasted, Sis. You never told me, or maybe not anyone? Jacky looks so much like you; it was easy to hide her father in her. But, since this is Halloween, can I ask...Is this a Trick or a Treat?"

Holly and Jacques looked at each other, their eyes already showing the retreat of misunderstanding and grief. Slowly, hope rose again, and with a smile, both agreed, "Let's go for the Treat."

TRANQUIL SUMMER TIMES

Lying stretched out in a meadow
arms folded under my head
gazing up into the blue sky, where
in constant motion,
a few frolicking clouds
transform themselves into
animals, castles and even fairies.
Perpetuum Mobile

Sitting on a shady porch.
lazily peeling a bowl full of apples
while a gentle breeze
complements the warm July sun
and carries the released scent of juicy apples
to entice a drowsy bumble bee.

Blowing the seeds of a fluffy dandelion head
watching them float through the air,
my mind too relaxed
to make a wish.

Wandering through a wide open field
far away from the busy world
Taking a rest against a sweet-smelling haystack,
left behind.
Just the two of us
in this vast, peaceful, domain.
The faint whistle of a distant train
the only sound to be heard

Emerging in the power
of ocean waves
crashing against rocks ashore.

Chewing on a blade of grass
letting the river take all thoughts away
on the crest of its gentle motions.

Feeling great inner peace
my eyes kissing goodbye
to the day's last sunrays.

THE LITTLE GUIDE

Her bare feet hardly made a sound
while plowing through the sand.
The path led through the dunes to where
the ocean meets the land.
Warmed by the sun, she reached the top
and paused. Wind tossed her hair.
In awe she watched the rolling waves
and breathed the salty air.

How wide, how free, this wondrous world,
majestic in its splendor.
The far horizon, endless peace,
just begging to surrender.
Her aching heart; to pause a while
and wash away her sorrow.
Then she could face another day
and not be mourned tomorrow.

She climbed the rock and sat down hard.
The waves below were pounding
"Wake up! Wake up! and listen well

our stories are astounding.
Through num'rous ages we survived
the brutal gales of winter
swept way up high, then pulled down deep
while ships get crushed and splinter.

"But we had faith in better times
when summer breeze is swaying
and we can gently roll ashore
delight in children playing."

She sat there for a long, long time,
her mind gone blank and weary.
Her eyes, while staring, didn't see,
her cheeks now dull and teary.
She's come to be swept far away
in merciful deep water,
yet still she sat here, motionless.
Ignoring waves who taught her.

A child's voice woke her from her daze.
It asked, "Why are you crying?"
She looked to see a little boy
who daringly was trying
to reach the top where she sat down,
despite a nasty tumble.
Then suddenly the world around
came back. And she felt humble

"Where is <u>your</u> owie? Are you sad?
My Mom can make it better."
He pointed over to the beach
where folks had fun together.
He offered her his chubby hand
and started the descending
she held it, scared he'd fall again
but thought, Who is depending?

A frantic woman came in sight
the boy ran to his mother.
She held him close. Glad he was safe.
The women faced each other.
"I'm so relieved" the mother said
"I thought that you were drowning."
"No" said the boy "this lady cried,
Please help her Mom." Then frowning
he looked from one face to the next
Mom slowly understanding.
Could see a smile break through the tears.
Now tears of happy ending.

"Yes, I was lost in grief and pain
and I'm so glad you found me.
Your sweet concern and guiding hand
did vanish all that haunts me.
You saved my life, though you don't know,
like waves, I was pulled under".

Then she knelt down and kissed the boy.
"Who sent you there, I wonder.

"My faith in mankind is restored,
you came and lit a candle,
its flame will always light my way
when things are hard to handle."

She waved goodbye, the sand felt deep
'twas far from easy-going.
But now she knew she'd find her way
when ill winds would be blowing.

A LOVE STORY

The car stopped in the parking lot,
A door swung open wide.
A cane emerged, but nothing more.
The old man still inside,
till slowly, very slowly,
he found strength to move his feet.
The cane assisted them to where
the pavement they could meet.
Now with great pain his body made
an effort to stand tall,
it took a while, response was slow
and then he heard her call.
His wife came shuffling 'round the car,
her slippers grinding dirt,
and so he waited patiently
for fear she might get hurt.
He offered her his still strong arm
she smiled at him with grace.
Then suddenly his back went straight
and pride lit up his face.

He was her hero, this he knew,
though bones were old and hurting.
She was his comfort and his joy,
her aging eyes still flirting.
And so they moved now, arm in arm
she in an old pink sweater
he trusting in his faithful cane
to bring them forth together.

I watched them go. I did not know
or see them until now.
But in my heart I saw their book
of life and love somehow.
It opened wide before my eyes.
What joy I felt within,
to witness this and find new light
to help my day begin.

THE ROSE

Old age is often frowned upon
the rose has lost its splendor.
Her thorns remain
with aches and pain,
a sad refrain
and all in vain.
Old age demands surrender.
Yet if we free our minds to roam
through years we left behind us
without regret
and only glad
for what we had
in good and bad
then happiness will find us.
For old can turn to gold again,
relax, take time, enjoy it.
Dwell here and there
with time to spare
so much to share
of love and care.

Pain cannot destroy it.
Don't wish to be that age again
the world has been a-turning
old minds can't meet
inventions beat
tremendous speed
of word and deed
with ever faster learning.
A happy heart makes spirits rise
the future to endeavour
each day can bring
new songs to sing.
Encouraging
the rose to cling
her fragrance sweet as ever.
Old age, a gift, a looking glass
relieved from haste and pressure
review again
all loss and gain
let hearts sustain
a new refrain.
Old age ... life's final treasure.

JULIA TURNER

Sorry!

Lost

The Cakeshop

Be Still

Captured Echoes

SORRY!

"Oh! Sorry!" I said, having inadvertently closed down a program on the computer.

"You don't have to apologize, Mum," said my son. It reminded me of what a friend had said a few years back: "You're always saying 'sorry'. It's annoying. Cut it out."

I was walking the streets of Dublin recently. One hears "Sorry!" constantly from people all around. They're apologizing for an accidental bump, or they're meaning "You go ahead in the queue," or they're pardoning themselves for taking a long time to find the correct change.

Entering Bewley's Café on Grafton Street, a gentleman stepped aside to give me room through the doorway: "Sorry," he said with a smile. On walking through to the back section where lunch was being served, I stood by the sign which said, "Please wait here!" After a moment, the hostess girl ran up: "Oh, sorry," she said, "We're so busy today." As I sat down one of my parcels bumped the table which was crammed beside mine. "Sorry!" I muttered, trying to be more careful.

Being in Bewley's brought tears to my eyes. I remembered going in there, as a little girl holding her mother's hand, all the way to the back where the wide, plush, padded, red velvet benches used to be up against the wall. I recalled climbing up onto the seat and turning around, finding my legs could just reach out to the edge. We had walked for miles, my legs were sore and the soft velvet felt blissful supporting weary muscles. My mother had said: "Never forget we have had tea here. And we'll come again. These walls know stories and hold memories."

"What would you like?" enquired the petite Polish waitress.

"Soup, Irish bread and a cup of Bewley's best coffee, please," I replied.

"Oh, sorry," she said. "We've finished up the soup for today."

"Too bad. I'll take an Irish scone and jam instead."

Drifting back forty years, I could see 18-year-old students arriving in the café in the middle of the afternoon, all talking at once, all trying to be sophisticated and all smoking the longest cigarettes available, jammed into even longer cigarette holders. What with skipping lectures, ruining our health with cigarettes, and drinking expensive coffee, none of which we could afford, it was a wonder we had survived financially, passed exams and remained healthy.

In Ireland today, Polish workers are well-trained and polite: "Here's your scone. Oh, sorry! The coffee has spilt a bit. I'll wipe it up. Sorry ... one moment." What good English she spoke!

I thought of my mother who had taken coffee in Bewley's in 1935, when she was 19. Afterwards she had written home to *her* mother back in Calgary, describing the experience in detail. She had known her mother would read the account over and over, remembering times when she herself had gone into Bewley's for coffee.

Drinking coffee in Bewley's is like going on a pilgrimage. The word 'Sorry!' and Bewley's Café are a part of my Irish heritage. I'll not be apologizing to anyone for spending time with either.

LOST

There was a certain excitement around our house that day, the last day of 1991, suspended between the Old Year and the New. A bottle of bubbly white wine was in the fridge for my husband, Ralph, and me, as we had decided to see the New Year in, at home. Our elder son was already at a long-planned sleep-over, with bags of chips, pop and video games, while our younger son was eagerly anticipating the arrival of *his* friend who would tote his sleeping bag and all the goodies boys of eleven might need for the celebration. Ralph was sorting files in the computer room, getting a head start on his New Year Resolution to clean out boxes of what our sons called "ancient stuff." The only member of the family that needed caring for was the dog, our big lab/blue-heeler cross.

It was just two o'clock in the afternoon when I laced up my hiking boots, zipped up my tattered buffalo wool sweater, knitted years before by my mother-in-law, and pulled on a brightly coloured toque to act as a warning flag to careless hunters. This time I planned to deviate from our usual trail. We would cross the creek. Adjusting the shoulder straps of a light pack, and stuffing in the rubber boots I would need to ford the creek, I reached for the dog's leash and called out, "Pepper! Time for a walk! Bye everyone! We'll be back soon."

These magic words caused the usual ecstatic leaping and barking, and the two of us strode out to spend some time together in the woods. I had first taken Pepper into the bush in the Fall, when she had grown into a strong six-month-old and needed long walks. She hadn't wanted to go under those trees. She had been fearful of water, until we had played many times in little creeks. She hadn't known about jumping and leaping until I had lifted her front legs followed by back ones, over logs, time and time again. Now she could clear all obstacles in one bound. Her confidence in the bush was supreme. There were signals we gave each other quietly, and she had on occasion warned me of "something up ahead" – a bear on the trail, or a cougar up a tree. We had turned away in time, avoiding a confrontation.

Today's unexplored trail held great promise. We quickly passed over familiar ground, where the sights had been memorised and the smells were predictable. In no time, Pepper was yapping and crashing in the creek. I slipped on my rubber boots, replacing them in the empty pack with my hiking boots. The creek was running swiftly, but it was less than a foot deep and the water would not get over the top of my boots. I studied the far bank: being very steep with loose clay, it would need to be climbed with care. By winding and working from side to side we could rise slowly to the top.

We crossed the creek and scaled the cliff. We turned right with the trail, to explore new terrain. There was beauty above in the branching cathedral canopy. This was untouched bush, pristine and lovely, even in winter. After a while, I realised the trail had petered out. It had been a good walk, and now it was time to turn around and go back. Already four o'clock, it had begun to rain. We struck out for home.

"Let's go faster now," I said to Pepper, taking longer strides across a flat grassy area. A few minutes passed, but we hadn't yet come back onto that trail. I was reminded of one of our computer adventure games. I wanted to press the "restore" button to be allowed to start over again, at the beginning.

I stopped to collect my thoughts. The rain was pouring down, but the water ran off my jacket. We'd soon be home and able to dry out. Speaking to Pepper, and urging myself on, I said, "We'll turn down here, find that creek again, cross back over and reach the path we've walked so many times before. Good thinking! We'll arrive home a little later than planned, then we'll order in pizzas; what fun it's going to be at home tonight – warm fire, cosy sofa and thoughts of the future ahead."

So we made the turn, breaking out towards familiar territory. We passed a couple of water-logged areas and noticed deer droppings in little piles on rotting leaves. I checked my watch: 4:30 p.m. "That creek *must* be here. And I *know* our path is beyond it! Now, where are they?"

We found the creek, but it looked different. Dusk was closing in. I considered walking in the creek, knowing it would lead to the trail we had originally used to cross the water. But there was danger if we stayed in the creek itself. One of us might slip on the rocks and break a leg. So we forded the creek again and strode up the bank. "It's quicker to follow the flow of water," I said over and over. "Don't try any shortcuts." Pepper kept close by my legs as though in agreement. I felt annoyed because I knew the pizzas should be ordered about now, and here I was, struggling in the bush. I certainly had misjudged the time. Would the kids have their chips out yet, or would they be too engrossed in their videos? Would Ralph have finished his cleaning?

I kept up a steady pace and was constantly amazed at the sparkling beauty all around. There was enough light to see large objects. I was confident familiar landmarks would appear at any moment. We had to veer away from the creek's bank as it rose to a cliff, and it was risky to stay near the unstable edge. The sound of the creek faded as the rain began to fall even more heavily. Suddenly it was dark. There could be wild animals nearby. I shivered, pulling back my sleeve to check the time again, but it was too dark; I couldn't read my watch. Perhaps that treeless area up ahead was the beginning of the trail? "Look to where it's light." It was brighter over there; a clearing, a beacon. It must be the trail! We moved towards it.

This was treacherous ground, there being so much debris on every side. I tested each step as a false footfall could break a leg. Unable to see my boots anymore, I moved slowly, struggling along. Eventually, we reached the clearing with a brighter sky, but open only because some trees had fallen in a wind. They had crashed down, the wind banging them against each other, giants smashing and shuddering. There was a great sense of the slow progression of time in that place. Enormous trees, silent as they died away, lying there stretched out along the ground; and then beside them, the growing trees, with their own timeless struggle upwards, seeking the light. Awed by the peace, I felt a need to share in it, to lie down and to go to sleep. On waking up, I knew I would be snug in bed, as always after dreams.

Pepper had crawled in under a log, scraping away the debris and circling to make a bed. She was so warm and dry. I tried to crawl in beside her, to fall asleep. In the morning light I'd know how to get out of this mess. It wasn't real. I would wake up any moment.

Pepper was having none of this. Was she talking to me? "Get up," she seemed to be saying, "Lick that face until it moves!" I dragged myself up, and half sat on the log. Deep darkness on all sides. The clouds above were brighter, reflecting a weak, diffused glow picked up from the lights of Port Alberni. Light in the tree tops, dark and black below.

Pepper, our S.P.C.A. pet, strong and energetic as usual, would never know the meaning of "Go home!" Her breeding told her that "home" is with her owner, and I was right beside her. But she stayed very close. I felt her broad shoulders lean against my shins. She understood there was trouble.

Now I realized I was lost in the bush. I might even be lost forever. I might die here. It was a horrible moment. I was not going to get out of this hell. My ears ached with the deafening splash, splash of rain on the flat leaves of the shoulder-high salal plants.

Then the low, dull sound of a jet, miles above us, reverberating, no doubt on its way to Japan. Half an hour after take-off, the passengers would be chatting and sharing jokes, having a drink, curling up in a blanket with a good book. No-one knew we were down here. No-one knew where we had gone.

I couldn't let thoughts of Ralph and the kids begin, as the guilt was too overwhelming. I stood up and called out, loud and long. My agonised yell came back wailing from all directions. I wouldn't try that again! I leaned against a wide tree, and the darn thing fell over. Although I knew falling trees can buck and kill, I stood transfixed as it sank down, down. I found another tree that stood firm, and put my arms around its strong, solid trunk. I gave it a hug; the rigidity of the wood helped. My mother always maintained that the women in our family have great inner strength. I had a job to do. I must keep focussed.

I was beginning to shake. It was beyond a shiver – my whole body and every organ in it was vibrating. Cub Leader training told me I should stay where I was. But I was so cold and my mind was going crazy. I *had* to move. But to where? Further away from the creek? The thought of falling off cliff banks helped us decide: we continued away from the creek.

With renewed vigour, I moved carefully, deliberately, safely. Warmth spread through me with the exertion, and I just knew the trail was going to be over that rise. But it wasn't. Maybe there was a homestead where that new clearing appeared? More downed trees. Was this a sawn off stump? Hard to tell, but if it was, that area ahead with fewer trees could include people, warmth, and lights ... another false hope. Each time I swung a leg over a log I had to coax Pepper up and down. She wasn't going to leap where she could snap a leg. We worked together, she and I, hardly stopping to catch our breath. She never wandered, and the few times I lost sight of her in a black patch, I panicked at the loss and snarled, "Here! Here!"

Pepper would move up, lean against me and we'd turn in a fresh direction.

BANG! BOOM! What was that? Oh, yes! The New Year's fireworks! So it's 9 p.m. From which direction is the sound travelling? The explosions echoed all around, bouncing off the trees. Which is west? East? Can't tell, but we mustn't slow down.

In time, we came to a new creek, far below us: a creek that shouldn't have been there at all! I had never heard of two creeks in this area. This one ran along the base of a cliff, through a black gully, and the roar of it was tremendous. The white foam flashed and rolled. I was totally confused. I couldn't even tell which way it was flowing. Maybe it was right to left?

Then I saw them, the Searchers. There they were, running up on top of that awful river in their yellow oilskins, flashing their huge search lights from side to side. They were shouting out, searching for us, and I was swamped with relief. This whole damn mess was going to be over.

Hallucinating, I looked for the rescuers again, but their lights had gone out. No! Wait! There they were, back where I had first seen them. They were repeating it all, running from side to side, to reassure me. No! They were gone!

Get a handle on yourself! Stay away from that crumbling edge. I backed off, before noticing some strange

Christmas tree lights that decorated the great, black firs on the far bank. They were gorgeous, hundreds of them in all the colours of the season. How could this be? I was losing my reason. Fear gripped my stomach, terror like wild animals must know. I've always followed my instinct when in a tight corner, and this time it told me to turn right around and stride out to where the first creek must be. Two steps and I fell down hard, the side of my face smashing against a dead trunk. It hurt too much. Pepper was all over me scratching and clawing until it stung. I pushed myself up. Below me was a thick dagger-long spike sticking straight up out of the trunk, three inches from where my face had landed. If it had entered through my eye, I'd be dead. Horrible! The shaking started again. Oh, God! Where are you in all of this?

Move! I must get up. But my thoughts overwhelmed me. Ralph and the boys must be in despair. I cried, and I asked, "Why is this happening? I can't do this. It's too hard." But I had stayed still too long, and the awful shaking was consuming me. Every part of me was rattling, vibrating and pulling in opposite directions. And it hurt: bones, organs, vessels. I could feel each one. I was sure they'd damage each other with the knocking about. I wasn't going to be able to get myself back together. I would soon burst apart. Explode! The End.

Pepper had crawled in under another log. I turned over onto my hands and knees to fit into her spot, but there was not enough room. I couldn't fit in. With arms around the log I heaved my aching body up and fell against the side of the bark. Despair took over. Beloved faces appeared before me.

My mind cleared, and I saw all the things we had done together. Good times, fun times, wonderful sights. As I watched, warmth flowed through my chest. It cleared my head, and I could feel it pass down my arms and towards my legs. A certain peace came and with it a feeling of calm. The rattling eased, a glow spread throughout, anxieties settled. It gave new confidence. I could call on this source of strength any time.

I reached down and pulled on Pepper's collar. "Time to get going." She leaped up, refreshed after her short nap, ready to go again. Wasn't this the greatest walk we'd ever had?

I remembered reading about the girl who'd survived a plane crash in the Brazilian jungle. She had followed flowing water until she found people, as she knew all trickling streams lead to the Amazon. I desperately wanted to get down to the raging waters below. I worried that I might miss the highway which must pass along the other side of this creek. Sometimes I could even hear the distant whine of trucks as they sped down into the Valley. I was on the wrong side of the water. I must cross over. Surprisingly, there was a logging road below, a dip in the cliff's side. I slid down, so thrilled to have some link to people. I jumped out onto the hard, levelled road with a great shout of joy, which died as I realised the ground had been scraped bare for only 30 feet. An enormous fir's roots had been torn up in a storm and blown down the cliff's face. Bare earth had been opened up all around. This was not a road leading somewhere! Tears stung my face, the salt getting into the scratches on my skin. I tried wiping them away, and smeared mud and grit across my cheeks.

Pepper had hardly paused by the roots, so I, too, began to zigzag down to the river. Hey! It was flowing right to left. Good! I had figured out something correctly. But there were steep banks on either side and we could go no further. Even logs hadn't been able to float on through this narrow gap. They were piled up high. Of course! Use them to cross over. Brilliant! I must be getting everything back together. I climbed and inched across. My feet kept slipping and breaking through the rotting wood. I could feel the racing waters tugging at my boots below. Each time, swinging by my arms, I dragged my feet up again. Then I realised that Pepper was not following, that she considered the logs too treacherous. I crawled back to her across the 50 foot log pile, and hooking on her leash I dragged her towards the river. I tried to lift her up but she was too heavy. She came very reluctantly, and I noticed her legs were shaking from fright. However, after a great struggle, and paw by paw, she did get over to the other side. I had got used to the monkey-like manoeuvres of arm swinging, and could concentrate on not losing my boots when grabbed by the churning current below.

Now, to get up that cliff. Halfway up, swinging on bushes and gripping roots, digging in with boot heels, I looked down and saw Pepper far below. She was barking, running to and fro, but her barks were being drowned out by the roar of the water. "Stupid, damn dog! She'd never been unable to do what I'd asked her before." Suddenly, somehow, there she was, in my face, licking hard. She'd found an easier way, she was just above me, and it felt so good to have a bit of warmth on my cheeks. It soothed the sores.

We struggled hard up the last part of the cliff, scratching, clawing and hauling ourselves over the top. We had got away from the noise and energy of the water. We were so tired, and Pepper half fell under a log. Immediately I heard her snoring, so I thought we should stop for a few minutes. I leaned against her log, in and under an overhang of 6-foot high salal. Exhausted and numb, tears were coming again. Oh, no! Not now! My eyes felt huge, wide as saucers, bigger than my head. They were growing all the time, stretching and straining to see in the gloom. My eyelids couldn't cover them. We had stopped long enough. I dragged out the dog by the scruff of her neck. She seemed half dead, but she struggled up on her feet and we turned to walk away from the river, at right angles to its bank.

I took a few steps and wobbled, my knees bending out of control. There was another log in front, the perfect height for us to sit on. This was meant to be. This was our place, a good haven, not quite so wet. Perhaps we could sleep. I felt dizzy. Was I going to faint?

Then a light flashed, but this time it was deep in the bush ahead. More torments. I'd rather try to close my bulging eyes. Another flash. Was Pepper seeing lights, too? She was draped across the log. I held her head in my cupped hands and I turned her head towards my lights. Nothing happened. No more lights; nothing for Pepper to see. She looked up at me, her eyes being the only part of her able to move. Then a light passed again. Pepper's body went taut and her ears pricked up. Another light? Pepper slid down off the log and stood rigid. Is this really happening? Could those be real lights? Hope surged strong. People! Run! Run! Hurry, before they're gone!

I held onto myself. No more lights in the distance between the trees. But look at Pepper. She knows something is there! Wait! Wasn't that one? Yes, there's another light!

About to run, I tensed up. "Don't jeopardise your chances by breaking a leg now." Step by step we inched forward until we came to a flat, mossy area. Here we could move faster. "Ralph, if only you could see us now. We're coming out. We're going to be okay. Everything's going to be fine. We're going to make it out of this awful hell. I'll be able to hug you all again. New Year's Day football on T.V. All of us together." I stopped and cried. I ached all over, the shaking was persistent, but it didn't matter. We'd be safe again. I clicked on Pepper's leash because here was the highway.

It wasn't the highway. There was no yellow or white line down the middle. But I did recognise Burde Street, and there would be houses down to the left. Perhaps one of them would have a hot toddy, an Irish coffee? The moment my boots hit the hard road surface, the skin of my feet split and tore open. For a long time the boots had been full of water, which now spouted out at every step. Legs were aching, knees were shaking – but what the heck? Here was a road, and soon we'd be safe.

A mile down the road, there were houses with real lights. My fingers couldn't straighten out to push in the doorbells. I pounded on the first door with my arm. Mud and water splashed over the white paint. No-one came. The doors of the second and third houses were not opened, either.

I walked on to where I knew there would be a public phone. A wonderful Italian man was standing out on the road. He took both of us into his home, in spite of my protestations, and gave the dog a drink and some left-over smoked salmon. He and his wife had been hosting a party, but now it was 3 a.m. and they were relaxing after having said farewell to their lingering guests. They insisted that I sit on one of their beautiful cloth chairs. We were filthy, and I daresay they realised it, but they insisted a chair was meant to be sat on. Water dripped steadily from all of my clothes, and off Pepper's fur, onto the kitchen floor. Our host gave me the phone to call home, but I couldn't open my fingers to push the buttons. He dialed for me. I was sobbing before I heard Ralph's voice.

Back home, Ralph had been seen by neighbours running up and down the street in short shirt sleeves, in the pouring rain, calling out my name. He had phoned friends all over town. "Did she come by for a cup of tea?" He had phoned the police to report a missing person at 8 o'clock, and the R.C.M.P. had responded immediately. The first to arrive at our house had been a policeman with a dog. Out they had gone on the trails, but they had found nothing, the heavy rain having washed away all scents. And no-one was sure where I had entered the bush.

Next came two plain-clothed policemen, who asked Ralph all sorts of questions: "Had we had a fight? Was I on medication? Was I depressed? Was I often out in the bush? What was I wearing? What shoes did I have on?"

The Search and Rescue Squad was called out, torn away from their New Year's Eve party. The car lights I had seen through the trees were those of the R.C.M.P. cars and the Search and Rescue vehicles speeding up and down Burde Street, manning the Search Centre set up at the top of the road. Beacons, they had guided us to safety.

I will never forget Ralph, as he came into that kitchen. To see him was what I had struggled for, through hell. We held onto each other for a long time, both sobbing, both knowing the outcome could have been so very different.

I spent an hour that night at the hospital, wrapped up head to toe in toasty hot blankets. I lay on a wooden hospital stretcher, and because I was still shaking so much, my back was bruised from banging on the hard surface. I wondered if I would shake right off the stretcher. Toes and fingers ached as they warmed up.

A policeman drove Pepper home, where our son massaged her shaking legs with our best bath towel. Later, the police drove us home and our son's hugs were treasures. All that long night our older boy had not been aware that anything had been amiss.

For about a week I feared the night, terrified a nightmare would bring me back to that awful place. I forced myself out onto the trails two days later, much as one does with driving a car after being in an accident. My right hand was stiff and crooked and needed support and medication. The side of my face was bruised for weeks. Even now, if I get chilled, that shaking begins and I do something, anything, to warm up fast.

It took the dry cleaners a week to clean the buffalo wool sweater. It had saved my life, as wool like that holds warmth, even when soaked and sodden. All my clothes had to be washed three times before the colours were recognisable.

Pepper slept in her kennel for the rest of that night, and for the whole of the following day and night, waking only once to drink some warmed up milk. She then emerged clean, ready for more adventures. It was her mistress who was tied to the backyard, preferring to dig in the vegetable garden than to test again her skills in the bush.

THE CAKESHOP

I was in Tralee, Co. Kerry, Ireland recently. Noticing women running in and out of the door of a house opening onto the street, I decided to run in too, out of the rain, and see what was going on. It was a home-style bakery. This is what was being said:

Hello, Mary, and what would you like?

Oh, I fancy a couple of those tarts.

All right! The weather's shocking, isn't it?

Oh, Jane, it's terrible, altogether.

It's gone beyond a joke. We'll all be washed away.

Oh, it's gone beyond a joke all right. Just look at it, lashing down again.

Oh, it's terrible. Terrible. Would you like anything else?

I would. You know, Tommie tells me them boat cakes are marvellous the way they taste so good.

Ah, yes. I fancy them myself.

Is that so?

Ah, it is indeed. How many would you like?

I'll have three. That way, we can all have one for our tea.

Ah, yes. And the weather's gone beyond being a joke.

Oh, it is. It's gone WAY beyond being a joke.

Oh, indeed. It's so far beyond a joke now. Honest to God! It's gone far, far beyond being a joke.

Oh, that is so, Mary. Way beyond. That'll be 7.50.

That's grand. Thanks very much.

Not at all. I'll see you tomorrow.

That you will. Tomorrow it is. And please God the weather'll be better then.

Indeed. Please God.

The cake shop lady turned to me and asked: And what would you like?

I was speechless with the sound of it all. I must have had my mouth open, for Jane said: Ah, don't be worrying now. The weather has that effect on us all.

I pulled myself together and managed to blurt out: I'll have one of them boat cakes, please. They look delicious.

They are indeed. Was it one you wanted? Right! The weather's terrible, isn't it?

BE STILL

Have you ever stood under a tree and been still? Smelled the bark and leaves? Watched what's happening under the canopy? Listened to the many sounds?

You can interact with the tree. Reach out and tweak a small branch, or run your fingers along some of the needles or leaves. Watch the twig bounce when you let it go. If a breeze comes up the tree will respond; it will move.

A tree has presence, unobtrusive and undemanding. But a conscious effort is required to notice such expressions of life.

Living things seem to project with greater strength when the light is fading. Although the following lines were written about a graveyard, the message holds a universal truth. It is in a graveyard that one is inclined to stop and pause, to look around and see. Poets write of such things:

The moon shone clear, the air was still, so still
The trees were silent as the graves beneath them. [1]

and:

Now fades the glimmering landscape on the sight,
And all the air a solemn stillness holds [2]

Stillness speaks volumes. Some people believe *to be still* is *to know.* When the word *still* is spoken, one might think of *Be still, and know that I am God.*[3] Written thousands of years ago, did the biblical songwriter feel there was too much noise and hubbub? Even back then, did *stillness* have to be requested? The lyricist was trying to convey: *calm down, and you'll know the answers.* In other words, *be still* and *calm down* go hand in hand.

A well-known bible story tells of Jesus being out in a fishing boat with his friends, when a great storm blew up. *"And there arose a great storm of wind, and the waves beat into the ship so that it was now full. Jesus arose, and rebuked the wind, and said unto the sea, 'Peace. Be still!' And the wind ceased, and there was a great calm."*[4] Waters raging, then the same waters *being still.* Like a mind racing, unable to sleep, for racing minds are as winds in the waves. Can responding to *Peace. Be still!* calm our waves and let us sleep?

---

1 Wordsworth (1796).
2 Thomas Grey, *Elegy Written in a Country Churchyard* (1750).
3 King James Bible, The Book of Psalms, No.46, Verse 10.
4 King James Bible, The Gospel according to St. Mark, chapter 4, verses 37 & 39.

Being stationary, not moving from one place to another, is the same as *holding still*. *Be still* and *hold still* mean the same thing. Shakespeare wrote[5] *Hold you still!* Today we might use instead "Shut up!" If we are to hold ourselves *still* we are to refrain from speaking, we are to make no sound. Is it not true that *a still tongue makes a wise head*?[6] In Ireland, I've heard it said, "He was a wise man, that James, a rare *still* 'un." This implies James had wisdom, but it could also mean James was not a bold man, that he thought before speaking and that he had a subdued, soft voice as well as a gentleness of spirit. He may have had the *sound of a voice that is still*.[7]

Karen Blixen wrote in *Out of Africa*:[8]

> Out in the wilds I had learned to be aware of abrupt movements. The creatures with which you are dealing there are shy and watchful, they have a talent for evading you when you least expect it. No domestic animal can be as still as a wild animal. The civilised people have lost the aptitude of stillness, and must take lessons in silence from the wild before they are accepted by it. The art of moving gently, without suddenness, is

5 Shakespeare, *Comedy of Errors*, III, ii, 69.
6 Hazlitt (1869).
7 Tennyson (1842).
8 Blixen (Isak Dinesin), *Out of Africa*, (London, 1954), 24.

the first to be studied by the hunter, and
more so by the hunter with the camera.
Hunters cannot have their own way,
they must fall in with the wind, and the
colours and smells of the landscape, and
they must make the tempo of the ensem-
ble their own.

To some of us, quiet implies the uneventful, a dullness,
a lack of action or sound. The best it can be is "a tedious
pleasure to the mind." However, *still* can also bring with it
a chilling of the soul. In 1811, Shelley wrote this line:

And from the black hill,

went a voice cold and still.

How grim is that? Makes the blood run cold. Rising
up with it is the chill of the lone, cold voice, the dread of
being alone, the panic of looming loneliness. There can be
much trepidation and fear for us if we are stationary, not
moving from one place to another, isolated, solitary.

Is it not restricting to have to *still* the tears and refrain
from weeping? How difficult is it when we cannot speak,
must compose ourselves, quiet our emotions, *still* our
grumblings? Perhaps we fear becoming *still* in the ultimate
way, perhaps death is right there. Do we not say a child
born dead is *stillborn*?

Religions and meditative societies know about stillness:

There was a deep and solemn pause
The monks stilled their chant [9]

A monk's chanting is an integral part of his life. To *still* his harmony is like stunning something beautiful to make it silent.

The act of *stilling* can be violent. In 1591, a cookbook contained a recipe:[10]

TO STILL A COCKE:

Take a red Cocke that is not too olde, and beat him to death, ... sley[11] him and quarter him in small pieces ... "

That would surely shut up even the wisest and oldest cock! The same cookbook describes a good housekeeper as *one who can preserve and still away well*; *to still away* means to extract the essence. In other words, she makes sure her preserves retain their wholesomeness and healthful appearance. This good lady can *still away the spirit, the soule itselfe.*[12] Personally, I would prefer to stay away from her, in case she got her hands on me!

We have many uses for this word *still*. Think of a *still* wine, how it is not sparkling or effervescent. A *still* is used in fermentation, and *still* is how a liquid is before it percolates and bubbles, when it is free from commotion, when it

9 Scott, *Monastery* (1830).
10 A.W., *Bk. of Cookrye* (1591).
11 *Sley:* to slay, to kill.
12 Donne (1649).

is quiet. At high tide there is a lull before the tide changes and the waters begin to recede. This brief, unruffled period is known as the *still*. Before or after stormy weather we might say, "The air is strangely *still*." Gazing into a dark pool of water, it could be said, "Here is a *still* pool. *Still* waters run deep." I have wondered about a stringed instrument which, although *still* and not being played, will make a lovely sound when the night wind travels through the strings. Wind instruments require air blown through to make a sound. Some wind instruments are called *still*-pipes and *still*-flutes:

The still-flutes sounded softly [13]

The still-pipes sounded a mournful melody [14]

Making still music to God [15]

Do we not say a stopped clock is *still*?

A clock that stands still is sure to point

right once in twelve hours [16]

Even time itself is said to stand *still*. And how often have you been surprised or shocked and found your heart was *standing still*?

A ship can be caught motionless:

The Ship stood still, and neither

stirred forward or backwards. [17]

13 Marston. 1602
14 Gascoigne. 1575
15 Fuller. 1642
16 Addison. 1711
17 Purchas. 1613

In 1861, Florence Nightingale wrote: *Many people seem to think that the world stands still while they are away, or at dinner, or ill.* Florence may have heard of the proverb: *Better to sit still, than to rise and fall* and maybe she knew of the bible quote: *And behold, all the earth sitteth still, and is at rest.*[18]

In 1874 an explorer noticed, floating in a bucket of water being carried from a well, a disc of wood a little less in diameter than the rim of the pail. "What's that?" he enquired, and he was told it was a *stiller*, a water calmer, a piece of wood placed on the surface of water in a bucket to steady it when being carried any distance.

Sometimes we, too, should strive *to be still*; for surely the pressures of life may be more easily managed, more calmly settled, when we *are being still*. The negatives should be let go, allowing the vacuum left behind to fill up gladly with positive feelings. When we read a book, we are *still*. To watch a play or a movie, to listen to a CD, to study a painting – all require us *to be still* before we can be aware, begin to know, begin to understand.

There is a German word *Still*, which may be translated as *calm, quiet, stillness*. This German word may be used with a verb to speak harshly to a noisy child, as in *Sei still!* meaning *Be still!* or *Be quiet!* or even, *Shut up!* In contrast, the word *stillen*, which comes from the word *still*, means to

---

18 King James Bible, Zechariah, chapter 1, verse 11.

nurse a baby, and conveys the peaceful warmth of a mother holding her nursing baby, calming the infant's crying.

One of our best-loved Christmas carols is *Silent Night. Holy Night.* The original words are *Stille Nacht. Heilige Nacht,* meaning *(It's a) Silent Night. (It's a) Holy Night.* While it does not ask us to be silent on Christmas Eve, it certainly evokes the calm peacefulness, the *stillness* of that night in the stable in Bethlehem.

When we hear *Silent Night* sung at Christmas, we can ask ourselves, *Have I been still today?* If the answer is *yes,* then we will have been blessed with awareness and calm. We will have cherished the value of silence. We will know. We will understand.

This old English writing was penned in 1534:

A tree hath a propertye to growe to a certayne heyghte, and whan he commeth to that heyghte, he standeth stylle.[19]

There is much wisdom and understanding to be gained from communing with trees.

---

19 Fitzherbert. (1534).

CAPTURED ECHOES

T-shirt, shorts and good shoes. Bow ties my thick hair. Racing through a late Spring meadow. I am fast and strong. Grass and flower heads bump my shoulders. Stalks prickle my face, bare arms and legs. Sweet smell of crushed clover flowers as feet speed on. Bright sunshine over everything. Bees whizzing; butterflies dancing. Sounds of children laughing ahead, beside, behind, inventing games of chase and hide. Oh, the joy of it! I could leap and dart like this forever. Stop! Plants, people, bugs might soon be gone. This golden treasure must be cherished. Exhilarated, spreading arms, spinning, I shout out loud, up to the treetops.

Bell bottoms, skin-tight shirt, long hair under green sunhat, sophisticated. I see the same field full of meadow flowers. Butterflies and bees, feeding or resting, I watch where they go. Kneeling, then lying in the grass. A soft bed. I look up at the swaying blades, bending in the breeze. And up higher, luxuriant trees whose spreading, mighty boughs roll slowly from side to side. Peaceful, unpressured. No-one needing my input. It's good to be back. I gather strength. A ladybug crawls and tickles: *go find your home and save your children.* Summer's end will come, soon. Breathing deeply, I seek each plant's bouquet. Rising up, I slide a stalk of grass through my fingers, pulling on the yellow clump at the top. Seeds scatter, landing gently, waiting for the following Spring. I sing, softly: *Remember Me.*

Pumpkin-orange sweatshirt, zippered tight against the dripping chill. I pull the sleeves over my hands. Socks wet, icy trickles seeping inside shoes. Dangling droplets on spiders' sticky webs. On short hair, too. Leafless trees spike into low cloud. Hint of smoke from unseen bonfire. Shapes and colours, dimming, slowly blending into inky black. Shadows creeping from under the trees. Light and dark boundaries closing. I pray: *Watch over my loved ones. Please keep them safe.*

Woolly hat, padded coat, layered sweaters. Cold-tipped fingers curl inside pockets. Gazing over the mist-shrouded field near Dublin. Ground hard, grass withered, flowers shrivelled, bugs dead. Damp cold grips my soul, ravaging memories. Am I strong, still strong? Crossing arms tightly to keep warm, I close my eyes to listen, to hear a child, any child, calling out. Silence. The sinking sun's pale reddish glow catches the treetops at field's edge. The sun is writing the script's end, as glory expires. Time has run out, the field has faded. Life has moved on, left me behind, sidelined by age. Tears fill my eyes. Turning away, I whisper: *Goodbye.*

> *Silently one by one, in the infinite meadows of heaven*
> *Blossomed the lovely stars, the forget-me-nots of the angels.*

LONGFELLOW

DEB OAKES

Together

You Know

Trail

Hiking The Cathedral Forest

I Ride

Cutting The Grass

Hairy Legs

Marshie

Thanks

TOGETHER

On a cold cement park bench, we sit together.

We're here in all kinds of weather, you and I.

Like two plastic ducks in an old millpond.

We sit here by the flowing water, we're not going any-
where.

As I gaze across the pond,

the purple heather lies close to the ground.

Here we sit, in sunshine, rain or snow.

Now with the cold autumn air the leaves flutter around us

The fiery orange and pumpkin yellow leaves

float from the tree as snowflakes flutter to the ground.

YOU KNOW

Your hair is like a sunset
The kind that brings to my mind the rhyme
    Red Sky at night, Sailors delight.
You know what I mean.

Your skin is like cream
The kind you used to get when milk was straight from a
cow
    Not the kind you get now.
You know what I mean.

Your body moves fluidly like water from a tap
Not like when there is air in the line
    and it spurts out.
You know what I mean.

Your smile is like a smiley face
The kind that brightens a person's day
    when life isn't going so well.
You know what I mean.

Your eyes are as bright as a glow stick
The kind you use to light up your tent in the summer
      Not like the sparklers our parents had.
You know what I mean

Your laughter is like tiny bells
The kind used on sleighs in winter
      not like the cow bells heard at sporting events.
You know what I mean.

Your memory will last forever like a scar cut into my flesh
just like the ones I have from the car accident
      that ended your life.
You know what I mean.

TRAIL

Trekking down the long and winding woodland trail
a snail. A common garden species,
making its way toward a pile of fresh bear feces. Through
the forest
I walked in August among the smallest ferns and tallest
trees
walking off the cream cheese I had for lunch.
A crunch and crackle behind me
froze my body in time, my heart raced
braced myself for what was to come my way
hoping I would be okay, with my breath held still
I was ready to kill; I slowly turn around and see,
a big grey squirrel running up a tall pine tree. He stopped
halfway
on this foggy cold damp day.

HIKING THE CATHEDRAL FOREST

It was Friday; I overheard fellow office workers talking about hiking through the many trails of Port Alberni. This weekend I decided to try something new. I wanted to fit in, join in discussions about trails, but I never go outside. I never get exercise.

Saturday morning was foggy. I felt the need to connect with nature, to ground myself.

I planned to go once around the trails in MacMillan Provincial Park, call my friend Raquel and join her for coffee. She's like me; she doesn't like to go play outside.

While driving to my destination, my cell phone started to sing. It doesn't really sing and I instantly recognized the ringtone I have set for my *besty* Raquel.

I looked at my phone, yelled, "Can't answer, I'm driving!"

Maybe I should stop and answer. No, I'm almost at the parking lot. When I stop I'll call her back. That way she can't talk me out of what I'm about to do. There will be no turning back!

I looked at the message; "What R U doing 2day?"

Is that all she wanted? I thought maybe she'd picked a new shopping destination or was calling with today's coffee shop location. I won't answer! She'll talk me out of my crazy outdoor hiking idea...

I answered, "I'm HtCGF"

She texted back, "You're what? Stop using text language and talk!"

Caught up with texting I typed, "O, I'm hiking the Cathedral Forest."

"No, you're not"

"OK, I'm not. I'm slogging through the rain soaked forest floor with trees surrounding me all the while wearing my gumboots and rain jacket."

The phone actually rang. When I picked up, there was wild laughter, "What the "H" ARE you doing? You **never** go outside. And you **never** go out on foggy days, let alone through the forest. Have you gone and lost your mind?"

"No, I don't think I've lost it, but seriously, I felt a great urge to walk through the forest. I heard it was full of old growth trees and such. Somehow, I felt today was the day, almost as if a tug from the universe was pulling me along. Guiding me."

"You should have asked me to join you."

"Really would you have? Or would you talk me out of the whole day?"

"Wait for me. I'll jump in my car and we'll explore the forest together. Then coffee! Maybe lunch! What do you think?"

"OK, I think I'll be here for a while, so if you are serious about exploring the forest.... Hurry!"

I left the cell phone in my car. On purpose.

As I waited, I looked around the parking lot. There was a massive tree right there! I bet Raquel and I together couldn't put our arms around it. We would need at least **six** more people. With six people we could stretch our arms out wide around the tree and hold hands.

Make a circle.

... A circle.

Circles are everywhere.

How profound.

Surveying the area I noticed there was a wide trail off to my left. I followed it, captivated by the trees growing before me.

The forest is mystical, magical, spiritual as the sunlight filters through the tree branches shedding an ethereal light as the branches tower over the highway, reminding me of a cathedral entrance. The trees, so tall.

Trees fallen on the ground birthing new trees and fungi... nurse logs, fallen branches.

Smell of forest... wet, earthy, pungent, woody, not pine but Douglas fir and Western Red Cedar.

River runs through it, elk tracks by the edge.

Fish going to the lake to spend their summer days.

Birds making nests in amongst the tree branches.

Trees so tall – ever reaching for the sun not quite getting there.

A breeze to keep the bugs from settling on me.

Raquel found me bound to the magic of the forest. She, too, was fascinated by the beauty of our surroundings.

Many people stop to walk these ancient forest trails to see the old growth forest for what it is – an amazing piece of Mother Nature at her best.

I RIDE

It's a long way to the top
      but it's worth it.
I ride my bike as far as I am able.
Almost to the top.
Train tracks are the halfway point.
going up the rough rutted road,
      I stop to catch my breath.
Inhale deeply, a breath of clean clear air
... fills my lungs.

I've ridden a bike since I was five
practicing in my own backyard. I ride up and down the
road
all day long.
Ventured forth to race the BMX track.
Six years old at the time.
Looking for more adventure.
To the hill I went and tried to ride.
      I rode.
         I flew.
            I knew this is what I should do.

I scramble on up to the top.

The Summit.

The Lookout.

I stand. Drink in the view of the valley, like the forest rangers before me.

To the west and to the east, look over the treetops and see,

the Alberni inlet

where freighters come to take away the trees.

I see Sproat Lake, Great Central Lake too.

Old growth forest beckons, young forest too.

I ride.

The thrill.

The rush.

The freedom.

Up the hill again

to not miss a chance to ride down again.

The cycle is complete.

I'm not alone; my full suspension bike known as

"The Bullet"

is with me.

My lime-green full face helmet protects my head.

Other pads shield the rest of my body.

While I ride the trails.

Dusk creeps in
      weaving in and out of trees.
Jumping roots and twigs
flying through these amazing woods.
The shade is cool, the sights whizz by
a puddle.
      Splash!
The air has a sweet, cool taste
on my tongue.

School tries to hold me in
my teachers, parents too
I long to be free
      to hit the trail
I long to *Be.*

The trails I ride are
aptly named:
Purgatory, a hell of a ride
      911, it's name should tell the tale
Gutwrencher's a bumpy one, don't eat before,
Don't forget Three Sisters, Scorpa, and Taco Loop.

The freedom, the rush
      is such a high
I'd think I've found my drug
to say, I'm high on the mountain
      Look out.

The rush I feel is really great
it's not for the faint of heart
carve the berm just right
   I am not alone
     See the line
Follow close,
   don't get left behind.

The trees. The ones they will take off my mountain.
I will not ride here for a long time now.
They have stripped the trees to nothing.
Left are the rotten, the old, the scrub trees to begin anew.
They wiped out the trails.

I will not ride here anymore.
I ride like the wind. It is in my hair.

They took away my mountain trails
They needed to cut it down
Dug big trenches cross the road
Tried to hold us off
It is their land
It is their right
but why should they do it overnight?

Please hear my plea
Don't cut the trees.

CUTTING THE GRASS

I listen for the rumble
as I watch Marty wander.
The lawn is mowed.
he strides past the grove of trees
shortening the grass.

I'm gonna cut the grass.
I yearn to feel the rumble.
To walk between the trees.
Time to push the mower, possibly wander.
I'll be so proud of the lawn I mowed.

It's not grain or hay to be mowed.
It's simply, our grass.
Remember to wear the proper gear.
As the motor emits its roar and rumble
I become mesmerized and wander
Toward the grove of trees.

Grass 'round the apple trees
needs to be mowed.

Got to stay focused, don't let my mind wander.
While I stroll across the grass
absorbed by the rumble.
Don't hit the trees
body pulsating to the rumble
as the lawn is mowed.
Stop to smoke my grass
I am apt to wander.

This will likely cause my mind to wander
run and hide my gear.
I'll smoke my grass
down by the trees.
Someone else ought to have mowed.
I hear my hubby grumble.

Now remember not to wander 'round the trees
Wear the proper gear as the lawn is mowed
Don't smoke no grass so you too
can experience the rumble.

HAIRY LEGS

Have you ever left your leg hair to grow long?
I tried last winter.
It crept way up past my thong.
Have you ever left your leg hair to grow long?
I knew it didn't belong.
Took to drinkin' liquor.
Have you ever left your leg hair to grow long?
I tried last winter.

MARSHIE

May is a great month to get outside after being holed up all winter. In Canada the first long weekend of spring is in May. It is the time to explore the big outdoors. Time to go outside. Matt, Julie, Steve and I made a pact last year – every year on the long weekend in May we would go camping at our newly found favourite campsite.

I rooted around in the storage compartment downstairs in my apartment building to find camping gear. Something had eaten holes in my tent. I added it to my list of things to purchase. Maybe I'll get a larger one this time. The rest of the gear was fine so I dusted it off and made a check list for groceries.

We car-pooled in two cars and could hardly control our excitement as we drove the three hours to the campsite. The site we chose had direct access to the lake. We would be able to set up our tents near the campfire and still be able to see the lake. There's nothing like lying in bed with your camp coffee watching the sun come up. The yellow orb seems to rise out of the lake.

"This is a great site. Let's make another vow to camp at this site year after year! Julie and I will put our tent on the left side of the fire pit," Matt said to the group.

"I guess that means Maggie and I set up our new tent on the right," Steve replied.

The two tents opposite each other should cut down on night noises. We put the chairs in between, near the fire pit. It still gets chilly at night in May.

We were famished by the time camp was set up.

"Hey Julie, do you want us to help with dinner?" Matt offered.

We were looking forward to the mouth-watering barbequed trout of the season followed by the ceremonial first roasting of the marshmallow.

Steve let out a big burp and said, "Julie, you did a marvelous job of cooking the fresh-caught lake trout. Who cleaned it for you? Better yet, when did you catch it?"

"Thanks, but don't kid yourself. It wasn't fresh caught and it didn't come from the lake," she replied. "The salad was scrumptious. Thanks for bringing that. I can't wait to see what you brought for tomorrow's dinner."

"Matt, I think you should light the fire, you were a boy scout weren't you?" I asked.

Steve, Julie and I pitched in with the clean up while Matt tried to light the fire.

"Matt you're sending smoke signals as if you need help. Do you?" Steve asked.

Matt replied, "The fire won't go. All the wood is wet. It's not my fault!"

"Where did you find such wet wood?" Julie asked.

"Down by the lake. I guess I shoulda got the wood they provide in the bin by the outhouses, eh?"

"Yeah, let's all go grab a piece of wood so we will have a fire big enough to roast marshmallows."

Clouds moved in and the temperature started to drop. Matt finally had the campfire roaring. The brightly colored flames were licking at the common crisscross pattern of logs in the fire pit.

"Wow! Now we won't be chilly. Did you know back in the cowboy days the campfire was kept going all night to keep the night creatures away?" I informed the group.

Sitting around the campfire warming ourselves, we became mesmerized by the bright blue, white and yellow hues we sat quietly reflecting our day. We were roused out of our stupor and brought back to the present. The flames had died down, leaving the coals a warm, red-veined with grey.

The first to break the silence was Matt. "Toss me the marshmallow bag," he said to Steve.

Matt caught the bag and tore open the tough plastic bag. He reached in to grab three of the bite size morsels.

Anticipation grew. "The first roasted delight of the season. Pass me one more and I'll roast one for everyone at the same time. Ya gotta love the taste of marshmallows roasted over an open fire," Matt boasted.

I was reaching for my own roasting stick when I saw Matt had successfully speared those unsuspecting marshmallows right through the middle. He really did want to eat the sweet treats as soon as possible.

Patience is crucial when roasting anything, especially when you do it over an open fire.

The soft white rounded cubes were crusting over. Light brown toastiness was creeping across the top. Matt was going to succeed. Imagine toasting four at one time!

Flames erupted and danced on the end of the marshmallow stick, leaping up the sugary confection. The marshmallows fell into the fire pit and burst into bigger flames. We jumped out of our chairs and stood there watching in awe as the marshmallows joined together and grew to double the size.

Julie giggled and made a joke about whether it would grow into a giant size monster and tromp over us as it went on its quest to rule the world. She really watches too much T.V.

The marshmallow grew until it was the size of a sweet potato. Not just any sweet potato, mind you, but jumbo size. The kind you find on the shelf in grocery stores around Thanksgiving. You know the ones I'm talking about, the ones Aunt Sally cooks up and tells you it's "delish" because of the toasted marshmallows on top.

We watched fascinated as an outline of a body formed. The marshmallow seemed to suck unburnt twigs from the edge of the fire ring and use them as legs. It stumbled, and climbed over the stone barricade that surrounded the rim of the fire pit leaving the warmth of the fire behind him. The marshmallow man fell out towards us. We nicknamed him "Marshie". He was no longer restrained by the fire ring! We felt panic was creeping in.

He was free!

Marshie stumbled towards our camp chairs. We grabbed them and moved them out of the path of the now intimidating marshmallow. Jumping onto the top of a nearby table we cowered and watched, terrified, horrified at how the marshmallow creature was moving along, making its own path.

Marshie sauntered towards the tents. Julie and I cowered dumbfounded. The boys yelled and made loud noises in an attempt to distract him, to deter him from reaching the tents. It didn't work. Onward he marched. In a matter of seconds Marshie had made his way to the bottom of **my new** tent. He was climbing up the side wall, spreading slime wherever he went.

As the marshmallow man climbed higher and higher he left a thickening streak of goo. His movements were getting slower with each passing moment. Marshie was beginning to slow in the cool night air.

I couldn't restrain myself any longer, "Stop! You're getting goo all over. I just bought that damn tent."

He didn't listen, but kept on solidifying, turning from the oozing melted mass he had become and spreading his sticky goo everywhere.

Minutes later I had grabbed my phone and tried to sell that tent on eBay. Cheap!

THANKS

Now the game is over

I'm glad you came to play.

Don't know what I would have done

the rest

of my day.

Authors

Photo by Alana Bodnar

The Desperate Writers of Port Alberni from Left to Right:

Anne Gijsbers, Deb Oakes, Margaret Growcott, Julia Turner

Printed in Canada